A Collection of Dead Men
nineteen short stories
1972-2017

By

Jacqui Jacoby

BODY COUNT
PRODUCTIONS, INC.

The author acknowledges the use of various trademark words in this work including and not limited to Greyhound, Budweiser, Google, Walmart, Sam's Club and more.

Library of Congress: 2016909462

ISBN, print: 978-0-9967678-1-1

ISBN, e-book: 978-0-9967678-2-8

First Edition, 2018

www.bodycountproductionsinc.com

DEDICATION

Everyone has their high school crush. My high school crush probably still carries feelings for *his* high school crush. They will forever be the cutest person you ever met, the nicest person. And thirty-five years later, if you are lucky and you run into them, they will remember your name, continue smiling and still be one of the nicest people who ever crossed your path.

I stand by my decision to lean on that locker in the upper hall in 1981. And I will still smile when I think of my high school crush stepping up and starting a conversation with me out of the blue…not informing me it was *his* locker I was standing in front of and he needed to get into it. He didn't utter a harsh word or a request to move. He was patient, talked nice and smiled a lot.

To All High School Crushes in the World, especially mine, I dedicate this to you to thank you for the happy moments in class and in the halls.

High School Crush with the Author, December 2016

ACKNOWLEDGEMENT

Editing by

Nas Dean

nas@nasdean.com

Cover Design by

Jen Connelly

justanotherjen@comcast.net

Readers

Amanda Shivrattan

Katelyn Sanchez

Lisa N Pollock

Liscia Renee Chavez

Travis walked out of the Dragon's Bridge Public House in New Orleans with Stuart in 1958. The plan had been simple: stay alive, leave everyone else alive and watch each other's back.

Quinn joined them in 1959

Jason in 1967.

With Evan's arrival in 1972, the house that had been a mere sanctuary began to take on the elements of more. The stories of a new generation of loyalties began to emerge.

This is The Dead Men's past.

For nine decades The Dead Men have moved in and out of each other's lives. They've hated each other, counted on each other and always found their place beside each other. Follow the history of the Dead Men as they find each other, one by one.

The Dead Men Diaries

Exclusively at

Facebook: Jacqui Jax Jacoby

Google+ Jacqui Jacoby

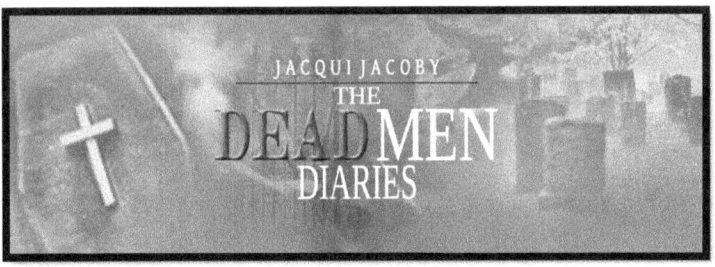

CONTENTS

Boy to Man, 1972

Two Too Many, 1974

Made in the Shade, 1979

Skin Deep, 1981

Wrong Place, Wrong Time, 1987

High Jinx, 1991

Good Night, Sweet Dreams, 1994

Seven Steps, 1995

Doctor's Orders, 1996

Collateral Damage, 1999

Cross Over, 2002

Brother from Another Mother, 2004

Meet Max, 2007

Yours, Mine and Ours, 2009

Late Good-Byes, 2013

My Sheets Are Blue, 2013

Rachel and Sarah, 2016

Power Shopping, 2017

Ho Ho Ho, 2017

Boy to Man

1972

They were in a house still new enough to have boxes stacked next to the walls. Travis ignored the shouts coming from the kitchen and stayed out of sight on the covered porch.

Bedtime had been hours ago.

No one noticed.

All attention was on the new member, the member who didn't want to be here.

Sitting in the lawn chair the previous occupants had left behind, Travis leaned forward, his elbows on his knees, staring at the photo in his fingers.

The kid in the picture had a smile on his face, sincerity shining in the eyes. It didn't matter that the photo was wallet-sized and small. There wasn't anything small about the look on Evan's face.

In color, four kids stacked shortest to tallest, were more members of the same family mix.

Evan loved them.

And Travis took that from him when they made him like them. It was only to save him; Evan would have died if Travis and Stuart hadn't been there that night. But shit, it hurt like hell to know they had caused this. They had taken a sweet kid and made him like themselves.

There were two holes in the wall of the hallway of this new rental. Evan had found some relief from his torment by punching his fist into the drywall. The kid was destruction on wheels as his new strength gave him an advantage he hadn't had before. His agony drove him.

Travis heard the door open behind him. Stuart stepped up and held the glass of scotch in front of Travis' face. Travis reached and took it but didn't drink.

"We're down another lamp," Stuart said. "Quinn cleaned it up."

"It's only been a couple of weeks."

"And a new city. And a new house. And everything so fucking new I don't think we're going to pull it off."

Travis leaned back and looked up. "Are you seriously suggesting offing a seventeen-year old kid?"

"Do you have any other ideas?" Stuart asked.

"You want to do it? Get rid of him for good?"

"No, but we have to realize we may be wrong. It might have been better to walk away from the situation. The kid is in agony."

Travis looked to the side. "What do you want to do? Stake him from behind? Maybe have Quinn slit his throat? Or just throw him outside at the right minute and watch him burn?"

Stuart sat down and silence reigned.

"You know I don't want that, but do you have any idea where we're going?"

"I have no idea what to do," Travis said. "Figured we would keep moving forward chance."

"He's too young," Stuart whispered.

"There are laws for us for a reason," Travis said, "I can't fathom ignoring them to kill a kid," Travis said.

More noise came from the kitchen. Shouts and stuff hitting the walls. Travis let out a heavy breath. Exhaustion dragged his shoulders down. Stuart got up first and Travis followed.

"It's not fucking fair," Evan screamed at Travis as he walked into the room. The broken remnants of dishes littered the floor.

Travis stood cool and calm while Jason stood up from his chair and Quinn stayed seated.

"We're trying to help."

"This is help? You turned me into this monster and you say you helped? It hurts," he said, holding his gut. "I want things and I don't know what they are but they're bad. You're bad."

"We can help you with that," Quinn said, pushing the glass on the table toward the kid.

"Your other option was dead," Jason said. "If the bastard you're talking about hadn't taken the chance on you, you would be dead right now. Drink this and you will feel better."

"I don't give a fuck what he did," Evan snapped back. "I want him to undo it. I want to go home."

Jason walked across the kitchen to the refrigerator. "You looked like a nice kid when we brought you in. Didn't expect you to turn into an ungrateful wanker."

Evan screamed and charged at the dining room table. Quinn snapped out of the chair, his hands up in surrender. Everyone jumped away a step.

Evan grabbed a high backed chair, swinging it, throwing it, and nailing the covered window dead center.

The window snapped, it cracked as pieces of glass shot toward the floor. The chair landed with a thump somewhere on the outside. The curtains came down, ripped and floating to the tiles.

The kitchen flooded in sparkling sunlight.

Jason and Quinn acted together. They each grabbed Evan by a shoulder, flipping him off his feet, slamming him onto his back and pinning the wailing kid on the tiled floor.

Travis felt the burn of the sun and knew they had seconds.

"Out."

Stuart sprinted first through the door, Travis stayed back and watched Quinn and Jason, still holding Evan by the shoulders, dragging him into the dining room.

Jason let go first, uttering a 'fuck' under his breath. Quinn held on a few seconds longer but eventually stood up, too. They stared at each other, a silent fury between them.

"Every one of us lost something and hated everything," Quinn snapped. "You get over it or you don't. If you don't get over it, you at least bury it and don't let it out to hurt the people trying to help you."

He turned around and walked to the living room and up the stairs. Bedrooms were on the second floor.

"There are no people here," Evan screamed. "Everyone is a monster and you turned me into one, too."

"You can call us whatever you want," Jason said. "We still didn't leave your ass in there to fry when we're so sick of your shit."

He headed toward the living room.

"Are you two okay?" Travis asked.

"Little singed," Jason said. "We'll live." He looked over at Evan on the floor. "But I think your new pet-project probably ran its course. Might be time to find a new home for him."

Stuart sat silently at the end of the bed, watching the kid in the dark. Evan's breaths were labored, his forehead damp with the pain of what he fought. He was so young and so lost and so afraid. It wasn't fury driving the behavior, it was fear. Evan lashed out at all of them. Craving blood could drive a man—a vampire—to kill the first person they came across. To beat back that urge took astronomical strength of will. Stuart didn't know if it was the kid that stopped that first kill, or the fact that four of them weren't going to let him near a door.

The only way to clear the path for Evan was to get him on the program. The rest of them were doing what they could to keep the faith, but that didn't guarantee success. Others had tried and failed. They had to get Evan on Ace in a Hole.

They would do anything for this kid.

Except give him blood.

"I woke up alone," Stuart said, soft with his Scottish lining his voice. "There was no one there to tell me what happened."

"I don't care."

"Aye, you do. You care too much. That's why it hurts. I lost my family, but they're more shades of pale grey than the bright red they used to be. You'll get there. It's going to take time."

"I want to go home. I want my mom."

"You can leave here and join a den. Become like the ones who did this. We can even help you find one if that's what you want. It's not easy but you talk to the right people and will find a direction. But you can't go home, I'm sorry. "

"The ones who did this to me, are they dead?"

"Would it make it easier on you if I lied?"

"You didn't kill them?"

"We didn't have the chance or we would have. You were down and we had to choose. Helping you was our main concern and them alive or dead didn't even matter."

"Feels like it matters," the kid said.

"Evan, you can be pissed. But you have to pull it in some. We want to help you. But you have to let us."

Travis heard Jason come down the stairs before he saw him. Sitting at the table, a cup of coffee in front of him, Travis felt defeat in all his nerve endings, causing a physical pain in his gut.

"I don't think your project is working out."

"I know what you think. I don't need to hear it."

"That's not what I mean. He used the phone in the den, wrote down the info then left without it. But he's smart. He should know better. If he was thinking clear he would have covered his tracks. He's not taking *Ace in a Hole* and he's not getting blood that I know of, so he might be firing from inside."

"What info?" Travis asked, looking up.

"Greyhound Bus. He called and got their schedule for buses to Seattle."

Travis glanced at his watch and did the math.

"Bus station is five miles at least," Jason said. "Even if he gets there in time for the departure, sun will be up when he's en-route."

Travis looked at Jason. "You want us to help?"

"I wouldn't wish pain on anyone. But we need to get him tied down and funnel the *Ace in the Hole* down his throat."

"Shit," Travis said, letting out a deep sigh.

"He's not upstairs. I checked."

Travis looked at Jason as Quinn came into the room.

"You let him go," Quinn said, "we're free of him and he makes his own choice. He probably won't though. Not unless he grabs someone and teaches them new manners." Quinn poured a cup. "Or you go get him and we keep trying. We do have a funnel in the kitchen."

Jason smiled and laughed a little. "Wanker did have potential, even if he was a pain in the ass."

Quinn drank his coffee hot and black. Walking to the cupboard, he pulled out a thermos and filled from the glass pitcher in the refrigerator.

"It's your call, Boss Man," Quinn said, twisting the top on tight. "You made the decision to do this. You're the one to end it. But unfortunately, you don't get a few days to think about it. That bus is leaving now."

Travis took three more sips of the coffee before he stood up. He swiped the thermos off the counter, went for his keys and walked out the back door.

He saw Evan on the road, a mile from the bus station, but he didn't stop. The kid looked miserable in the rain so Travis kept on driving. He parked and got to the Seattle departure gate well before Evan made it.

Travis waited in a black fake leather chair and stretched out his long legs. He saw Evan buy the ticket with money he had to have stolen from one of them.

Travis saw the kid see him. Evan stopped mid-step to stare before looking at the ground. Travis looked at the window in front of him, seeing the bus that would take him away.

People moved around even at this early hour, most looking like they wanted to be anywhere but here. Rain hit the windows in silver spots. Travis just sat in his chair.

Evan came over to slink down next to him. Water from his hair dripped down to his face, His clothes stuck to him.

"You're going to make me go back?"

"No. It's your decision. We showed you as best we can what we have to offer. If you don't want it, then you get to go.

A lot of what you are going through, though, will get worse. The pain and the fury. It doesn't stop until we make it stop."

"How do I stop it?"

"Three ways. You wait for sunrise and take a walk. Or, you can wait in the shadows until someone comes too close. Feed on blood and all of this goes away in a heartbeat."

"What's my last choice?"

"You follow us. It's hard, but we know what we're doing and can fix it with just a little time. It doesn't take much to start the process and feel better pretty quick. If you listen. And trust."

"You want me to trust the man who did this to me?"

"The only thing we did wrong was make a choice and that choice resulted in you still breathing."

"It's not fucking fair," Evan said, his voice deep with emotion.

"No, it's not. And I'm not going to bullshit you with how it happened to us and how bad we had it because we did, some in worse ways than this, if you can imagine that. It fucking sucks. You're right."

Evan looked at him. "I don't want to do this. I don't want to hurt anyone."

"Evan, you get on that bus now, they find a pile of ashes in the back before you are halfway there. The trip is too long and you can't hide from the sun."

"I don't care. I would have tried to get home."

"Who's going to know when you're dead?"

Evan leaned forward and put his head in his hands. "My head hurts. It never stops. I see things and hear things."

"I know."

"They needed me. They needed a big brother. My mom is crying right now. My dad, he's probably in the garage rearranging his tools like a zombie."

"A hundred years ago I fell off the map for mine. I never saw any of them again. I never visited the land we had or checked to see if they remembered me. I moved on. I became something bad. And then I became something good. My parents and brothers, they were victims, too. We have to accept that. We hate it but we move forward."

"Thanksgiving is in three weeks. I've been carving the turkey for three years. I want to carve the fucking turkey and eat mom's cranberry sauce and have pumpkin pie."

"We'll have a turkey. You can carve it and I'll take a shot at cranberry sauce. You can be as unthankful as you want, but you do it with us from now on. That's just the way it is, Evan."

"Why?"

"Because we're your family now and we'll fuck-up and make your life miserable at times. But we will never give up on you and we will help you in any way we can."

"Cut Stuart's hair," Evan said, trying to joke with sad eyes.

Travis smiled. "I am afraid there are some things in this universe even we can't do."

"I want to go home. I want to go to school. I don't want to do this."

Travis put his arm up, pulling Evan into a half embrace. "In ten years that feeling might subside a little. Probably not much. In twenty-five, you'll be one of the lucky ones who still remember being human and can still appreciate your loss. At some point it won't hurt so much and you'll only remember the warm glow of what you had."

"Can't I just have it back?"

"No. I'm sorry. And you can't go back, you can't see them. You can't have anything to do with them ever again. You won't even be able to visit your own grave."

"I have a grave?"

Travis nodded. "With the blood and the jacket found the police closed your case. You're not missing anymore. You're presumed dead. Jason found the report when he called the police in Seattle."

Evan looked down, then back up.

"Your parents had a place picked out for you and buried a coffin." Travis said. "Usually it's full of a lot of your shit. Like they needed something to hold and remember with. The tombstone will be up in a few months. Jason will track down a photo of that, if you want."

Evan looked at the ground. "There was this girl," he said. He looked up at Travis. "Donna." He looked back down. "She liked to go to the games. She would cheer us on and smile." He tilted his head up. "I liked her but I was too afraid to say anything. I was working up the nerve to ask her to prom."

"Prom is five months away."

Evan smiled a little and cocked his head. "It takes me a long time to work up the nerve. I can't see her again, can I?"

"My girlfriend's name was Jeannie. I liked her. A lot. I don't know if it would have gone much further but I was having a hell of a good time finding out. She's dead now. We never had our chance."

"Doesn't that piss you off?"

"Used to. Hated the person responsible for taking that from me. Then it just dawns on you one day. We got dealt a shitty hand and we stand back and think about that all the time, or we adapt and realize that even the bastard that did it, maybe he can be a friend."

"You did this to me, didn't you? You're the one that actually did it."

"Yes, technically I did. The circumstances, though, would you rather not be having this conversation and be in that grave because that's where you were heading when we walked up."

"So I thank you?"

Travis shrugged. "I don't know. Maybe somewhere in the middle. We're not monsters and we have room. Everyone likes you and wants this to work. You should really consider coming home for breakfast. We still have a lot of *Ace in the Hole* and you should try it. Sun will be up in a couple of hours."

Evan turned his face to the front and Travis let him have his silence.

The minute ticked by. People moved back and forth.

The Seattle bus pulled out of its berth and they watched it drive away.

Evan took the bottle offered by Travis.

"Will I ever feel normal again?"

"No," Travis said. "Everything is different from here on out, but different doesn't mean bad. Some days we might even venture to a movie."

"Monster movie?"

"We can do horror."

"And we get popcorn and Milk Duds?"

Travis grinned. "You've been talking to Stuart. That's his favorite order."

Evan turned his face toward him and that was almost a smile. Looking back at the bottle in his hands, he twisted off the lid and took a long drink.

Travis sighed, smiled and stood up. He put his hands in his pockets. "Come on," he said, nodding toward the parking lot. "Let's go home."

Two Too Many

1974

Saturday Night

Poker games only came a couple of times a year. Set on a night when no one had work or a girlfriend commitment, the time betting and counting chips relaxed the crowd while reconfirming a history that said they could beat each other's ass.

That history right now was a deck of cards, a stack of chips and varying kinds of bottles being passed. Vampire and drunk was hard to achieve. Vampire and 'damn I'm feeling good,' was easier.

The thick smell of expensive cigars hung in the air. In the living room, their stereo played The Doors.

"You guys are morons," Evan said, leaning back in his chair, his shoulders slumped.

Quinn smiled. The baby of the family could pout just right when he wanted to.

Jason stared at his hand, pulled the cigar out of his mouth to blow smoke above their heads. "This from the guy who lost the last five hands."

"Least I don't have your kind of woman problems," Evan said, staring at the pot.

Quinn smiled at the jab, his own cigar in his teeth. He stared at his two pair and debated whether it was worth it to stick in the game. Five card draw didn't leave a lot of wiggle room and fours and twos might not be worth fighting for. Picking up his chips anyway—three blue—he tossed them into the pot.

"The problems I have with women," Jason chuckled, "you can only hope for." He matched Quinn's bet and raised. Stuart went next.

Evan laughed and tossed his cards face down.

"Don't," Stuart said as he stared at his cards.

Quinn saw Evan fold his arms and sulk.

"Don't what?" Quinn asked Stuart.

Stuart's smile held tight and he tilted his chin. Bracing his arms on the table, he looked to be trying to hide behind his cards.

"*Jaaason*," Evan said, dragging the word out long. "What's the name of the girl you're seeing right now?"

Stuart slapped his cards down and groaned.

Travis kept fanning his. "I think it might be nice to live alone," he said as he pulled out two cards, putting them face down on the table.

"That was a good game," Stuart said to Travis. "I think I might have won."

"Carol Anne," Jason said. "Why?"

Quinn let the name settle over him then began to think of the implications, not really liking anything that came to mind. He chuckled a little and lowered his cards, to stare at Jason. "You're dating a girl named Carol Anne?" he asked.

Jason's gaze left Evan's and came up to Quinn's. "Yeah, couple of months now."

Quinn narrowed his eyes and pursed his lips, letting the obvious sit between them. "Not a common name. Sounds like a name you might inherit from an old aunt," he said.

"Okay," Jason chuckled.

Evan smiled while Stuart got up from the table and headed toward the refrigerator. Travis leaned back and braced his hands on top of his head.

"It *was* a good game," he muttered. "And I would have beaten you, Scotsman."

Quinn ignored Stuart and Travis.

"My girlfriend's name is Carol Anne," Quinn said. "Has been for about a month and a half."

Jason took the cigar out from his lips. "We both nailed the only two Carol Anne's in Seattle?"

Quinn slapped his cards down. "I'm thinking no."

Jason stared for only a few seconds. "Ah, shit," he sighed, his shoulders slumping, his cards hitting the table. "Brown hair?"

"Yeah."

"Brown eyes?"

"Yeah."

"Little strawberry shaped birthmark on her—"

18

"Yep," Quinn moaned. "Damn." He looked up at Evan. "You're a brat. You know that, right?"

Evan laughed and went to the kitchen for another beer.

"Radio Shack?" Jason asked.

Quinn shook his head. "Produce section of Queen's Market." He raised his gaze to Jason. "She wanted to know if her melon was ripe."

In the kitchen Evan covered his mouth and snickered. Travis controlled his laughter with a tight smile.

"How did you know?" Quinn asked the rotten kid.

"Because you're both losers. Both of you came in on a Sunday–different Sundays—and told me about this amazing chick and what she did for you. Made me promise not to tell."

"You told," Jason said.

"Of course I told. About ten seconds after you fell asleep." Evan laughed harder.

"And no one said anything," Jason said, pointedly looking at Travis, their fearless leader.

Travis shrugged. "Never actually had this problem before. We kept hoping one of you would bail and the other would never find out."

"Because we do secrets well in this house," Jason almost sneered. "That's harsh."

"Like I said, we've never done this before. We weren't really sure what we should do."

Jason looked at Evan. "She was available because her Mom was out of town."

"Her Mom died four years ago," Quinn chuckled.

"Maybe she didn't know she was seeing both of you," Evan offered behind his smile.

Stuart snickered. "She might not know that you two know each other but she damn well knows who's been heating her sheets and she knows there's more than one. You haven't seen a third hanging around, have you?"

Jason stared at Quinn then Jason picked a quarter off the table and polished it with his thumb.

"Flip for her?" Jason almost smiled.

Travis just about barked his laugh. "Classy, Irishman."

Tuesday Night

Jason's specialty was play. He could wine and dine a girl and make her feel like a million bucks and he did it with charm and sincerity.

In for the night at Carol Anne's apartment, Quinn smiled when he went into the tight spaced kitchen of her one bedroom. It was a nice place in a nice neighborhood that her nurse's salary could afford. The furnishing was wicker with macramé hangers holding her plants. It smelled good here, he thought. Strawberry and vanilla even when there was no source.

They may have met at the store, but he had first seen her in the children's ward where he worked as an orderly. Carol Anne had pulled out a sock puppet, talking through what looked like a toy monkey while Quinn had watched un-observed. The kid had laughed, his fear stilled while she walked with the wheelchair to the other room.

He liked compassion; he liked to see it radiate off a girl's face like it did Carol Anne's. It hadn't taken too much for her to talk him into a date and then bed.

He liked her. He liked her a lot.

Reaching into the refrigerator, he pulled out two beers while staring into the big plastic garbage can and seeing the tell-tale bag from the ice cream store up the street. The two large cardboard dishes on top still had the remnants of chocolate fudge on the inside.

He liked her a lot but he wasn't sure he liked sharing her with his best friend.

Quinn stared at the mess in the can, smiling a little as he got the bottle opener and took off both caps. He threw them on top of the leftover ice cream, figured Jason had chocolate ice cream to go with his fudge sauce because that is what Jason always did. Quinn grabbed both beers and headed back to the sound of the TV.

Thursday Night

Quinn was a handyman around the house at home. When something broke, even Jason might ask him to help.

Jason sat in the chair across from the TV, looking at the shelves that hadn't been in Carol Anne's apartment before and took a swallow from his beer. His smile felt infectious. Three shelves ran on tracks on the sides. They already were decorated with plants and photos.

He looked over at her, watching *The Carol Burent Show* and used his grey matter to line up all the facts.

It wasn't hard.

He was seeing his best friend's girlfriend and didn't know what to think of that. He and Quinn were as close as two people could be and that would always take priority.

He met her two months ago when he was buying the new Diamond replacement needle for the stereo, she was looking for a new clock radio.

She gave him glances and smiles. Then she brushed his arm as she moved by him.

It was the laughing at his stupid 'neuron walks into a bar' joke that was the kick off.

He liked the way she looked, the confidence of a woman aware of her beauty without flaunting it. The sensuality he had suspected in the store had been confirmed just two days later when they became lovers.

He liked her.

He liked Quinn more.

"New shelves?" he smiled into his beer as he took a drink. "You should have asked," Jason said. "I could have installed it."

Carol Anne looked at him, her big brown Bambi eyes blinking at him with pure innocence. She looked at the shelves and back at Jason. Jason required honesty in his relationships. She had lost him with the lie alone.

"I didn't want to bother you. We don't get much time as it is."

Sunday Night

Quinn came down the stairs with a hop to his step even though he didn't think he totally felt it. In three weeks, no quarter had been given. The double jeopardy in his love life, still remained floating somewhere above acceptable.

The thing was, he couldn't really be mad at Jason and that was annoying him the most. It was the seventies, he told himself. The *Joy of Sex* was on bookshelves. People lived together without marriage when he still remembered what it was like to be committed in a relationship.

"I wouldn't," Evan said from the table, his face planted in his book, *Do Androids Dream of Electric Sheep?*

Quinn stopped short of the door and turned. "Why not?"

"I'm thinking it probably won't be worth your time and it could get embarrassing."

Quinn rolled his tongue in his cheek and looked around the room. "Jason," he half smiled.

"He left about twenty minutes ago while you were in the shower." Evan didn't look too put out by being the messenger.

"It's my night. I had the date with her."

Evan's grinned annoyed Quinn as much as Jason's departure.

"He called the florist from that phone right there," Evan smiled as he pointed. "He wanted to make sure the order was ready. It sounded like a big fucking order."

"Florist," Quinn growled. "On my night? That's not playing fair."

He stood in the kitchen for another couple of minutes, watching Evan go back to his book. Quinn was pretty sure Evan wasn't really reading. Quinn was also sure someone should take care of that smile on the brat's face.

Instead, Quinn made popcorn, picked up the *TV Guide* and sat with Evan watching *Kung Fu, The Six Million Dollar Man* and *Night Stalker.*

Evan went upstairs and Quinn stayed watching the TV until late into the night. The channel was obscure and independent but provided some brain numbing benefits.

He heard Jason pull up his too-small-sports-get-up into the drive. Quinn looked at his watch, then went back to the garbage on the screen.

The door opened, it closed and Quinn heard Jason come up behind the couch where Quinn was stretched out.

"That looks good," Jason said with a sigh. "High standard viewing."

"It's three in the morning. Not a lot of choices."

"You'd be surprised," Jason said.

"I don't think I want to hear about it."

Though to be honest, Quinn wasn't pissed. Annoyed, but not pissed.

"I got her lilies," Jason chuckled.

Quinn's gaze jumped up to Jason's.

"Yeah," Jason smiled. "It took the florist days to pull it together and cost me a fortune but it was funny as hell when I got there with four dozen and she didn't have a clue what to do about it. Roses, she said. It was normal for a boyfriend to bring roses. My original plan had been to take them over yesterday, but the order was held up. I guess a lot of places don't carry that many lilies."

"Four dozen lilies?" Quinn laughed.

Jason smirked and nodded.

Lilies, representing death in the vampire culture.

Quinn sank back into the couch as he laughed. "I'm sure she was grateful," he said.

"I don't know if she was or not. She never got the chance to tell me. There was a guy in her bedroom closet. It wasn't his night either."

Quinn stared at the TV, not seeing the picture and laughed."How did you know?" Quinn asked.

"Besides the Old Spice? He had a cold. Kept sneezing and trying to cover coughs. I pretended not to notice and stayed right where he couldn't get by me. She was so damn flustered and I pretended not to notice."

Jason came around the couch, bumped into Quinn's legs resting on the table. Quinn picked them up, let him pass and Jason plopped down. He reached over, picked up the popcorn bowl and ate the leftovers.

"So you were screwing around in her room with #3 in the closet?"

"Naw," Jason said, setting the bowl down. "I just kept saying I was too tired while listening to him sneeze." He smiled. "It might have actually been better than sex."

He looked at Quinn. "Though to be honest, my interest in carnal knowledge with her waned about the time Evan folded his shitty hand of cards. Just didn't feel right."

"I liked her," Quinn said, looking at Jason. "Not a 'let's go steady, here's my pin', but I liked her."

"Yeah, I know. She was fun when she was fun. I actually thought all those nice qualities were part of her character and not just the entrance fee. I didn't see any long term there, but when you know for a fact she is seeing your best friend and playing it, lilies are in order."

"I gave up the sex, too. Made out a few times, but didn't go any further. Even that felt wrong."

"Didn't seem to bother her too much."

"She knew?" Quinn asked. "About the two of us?"

"She kept a diary in her nightstand. I think all the gloating she did in it was part of the replay for her amusement. I found it there weeks ago. Tonight when she was in the kitchen getting drinks, I took a shot." He reached into his inside pocket and pulled it out.

"You shit," Quinn laughed.

"I'll mail it to her later. I just wanted to know how far she would take it. How surprised would you be to find out we weren't the first?"

"Shocked."

Smiling, Jason opened the book to the last pages. "She thought you tasted better but me, she liked the playful shit in and out of bed."

"Immaturity," Quinn smiled. "Your strong point."

"But Mark," Jason pointed at the book, "His name is Mark. He was all around better in bed and everywhere else apparently, though," he looked closer at the page. "Dolt. She said he had a big fat wiener but had the personality of a dolt."

26

Laughing, Jason looked up.

"Big fat wiener? She said that?"

Jason held the book for Quinn to see. There it was, in her tiny flowery handwriting.

"And big fat wiener trumps a dolt?"

Jason's humor waned, his face taking on the edge of serious not usually seen. "She saw us together at the White House Bar a while back." He held up the book. "It's in here. She was interested in both of us because we were so different. Her words. She couldn't decide which she liked better so she tried both, making us two of the most gullible idiots to date."

"Chicks got energy."

"Does she get to walk on this?" Jason asked.

"Do we care one way or another?"

"We could scare the shit out of the two of them late one night, sneak in while they're asleep with capes or something."

Quinn laughed and leaned back. "I think I'm good. I had fun with her and it was never going to go further. Let her amuse herself with her big fat wiener."

"She used us," Jason pointed out.

"Maybe we used her."

"What do you mean?"

"These last three weeks, were you having more fun not sleeping with her, or leaving ice cream bags at the house for me to find?"

A grin split Jason's face. "Never thought of it like that, but yeah, I barely thought about the sex at all. It was more fun seeing what she was going to do next."

"You know this free love shit, now?" Quinn asked.

Jason looked at him but didn't comment.

"Used to be more fun, I think. With the challenge of meeting and getting to know someone. Then the sex was good."

"You're not into biology?"

"Are you?" Quinn countered.

"Carol Anne has her Mark. In six months one or both of us will have someone to talk to. I think we'll be fine as long as we're more careful."

"Or not," Quinn smiled.

Made in the Shade
1979

Parties lasting all night, didn't last as long for the guys enjoying the fun.

Bonfire on the beach, the orange glow on the lake a dozen feet way. The smell of water and hot dogs and smoke made the senses crave more. Cars were parked to the south. People dancing to the Boom Box, to the north. There were almost fifty people here ranging in age from 'don't drink that', to 'I'll never tell'.

Quinn took a sip off from the aluminum can marked Budweiser, thinking the beer wasn't too bad. And tonight, with the amount he had consumed, he might even be considered buzzed with that warm feeling in his head.

It was surprising how many kids came out to party on the shores of the Idaho lake this hot, muggy July. Jason had disappeared over an hour ago with a redhead. Weird, Quinn thought, taking another drink. Jason usually went for blondes or brunettes.

Evan took a break from dancing around the fire with his own brunette…and a blonde. Go Evan, Quinn smiled. They didn't let the little guy out much, but when they did they wanted him to have a good time.

Laughing, Evan came back and looked at his watch. "Where's Jason?"

Quinn pointed toward the parking lot. Evan's gaze followed.

"Oh shit. Does he know what time it is?"

"You want to go figure out which car he's in? Knock yourself out. Not sure he'll be happy you found him."

"Quinn..." Evan whined.

Quinn leaned over and reached in the ice chest pulling out another can, handing it to Evan. "Have another beer. We've got almost an hour until sunrise. He won't miss it."

And he didn't.

Ten minutes after Evan drained the can, Jason walked back up the beach with his arm around a pretty lady. He whispered in her ear and she smiled. Jason kissed her on the cheek and let her walk away, watching as she swayed in a short skirt.

Quinn watched, too. So did Evan.

"All done?" Quinn smiled, turning toward Jason.

Jason smiled and said nothing because a gentleman wouldn't.

Evan punched him. "You son-of-a-bitch. I hate your fucking guts."

"I know you do," Jason smiled. He looked at his watch. "Is there a reason we're not heading toward the car?"

Quinn checked his own watch. They were thirty minutes from home. "We're good."

Moving to the parking lot, they found Evan's new toy at the far end. Evan was teaching himself to rebuild cars. He had practiced on a couple of others, selling them when he was done for upgrade money and tools for the garage.

But Evan was keeping this car. It was a 1972 Challenger.

He even named her.

Peggy.

And Peggy was right where they left her, but something didn't look quite right.

Evan moved fast. "What the—"

He ran around the car, checking all four tires, finding the flat in the back.

Seeing a potential problem, Quinn's gaze shifted toward the horizon while Evan knelt down in the dirt.

"I'm thinking this will fuck up our timing some," Jason said.

"You have a spare, right?" Quinn asked.

"Yeah," Evan said, poking at a hole in the tire. "I'm not an idiot."

But he was a kid who hadn't finished rebuilding his prize.

Quinn and Jason got the jack, the iron. Then the three of them stared at the tire with rust so stiff that three super strength vampires couldn't get the nuts to budge.

"What will work?" Jason asked. "What about Coke? I heard that once."

"It works but takes days. And this tire is not coming off."

Across the lake in a breathtaking show of color Quinn hadn't seen in decades, the edge of the hill began to turn light, meshing into pink.

"I think a Plan B is required," Quinn said. "Now."

Jason looked back and forth, then looked at the open trunk. He looked to Evan and Quinn saw the wheels turning.

"Even if he fits," Quinn said, "we don't know if it's light proof and certainly not heat proof."

"You're going to put me in the trunk?" Evan snapped at Jason. "You're going to fucking put me in the trunk?"

Jason tilted his head at the challenge and stepped forward.

"Plan C," Quinn said.

Jason stopped and looked at Quinn.

"Options?"

"One of the other cars?" Evan said.

"They all have windows," Quinn said. "How about a dock, under it? A cave? Shit there's got to be something around here."

"I saw a shack," Jason said. "It didn't look too good but it had four walls and a roof."

"We're out of time," Quinn said, pointing at the dawn. "Jason, grab the six-pack."

"It's a five-pack," he leaned into the front on the passenger side while Quinn riffled the backseat, looking for anything that might help and finding nothing.

Quinn came out of the car first, empty handed. "Lock it up."

Evan looked at the horizon as they headed down the shore. "We're not going to make it," he whispered.

"There," Jason nodded.

It was closer to the hill than the water, a wooden shack erected long ago. They jogged the distance.

Quinn opened the door. Jason, still holding the five pack, pushed Evan in hard.

Quinn pulled the door shut and secured the lock against any accidental openings.

"Fuck," Jason muttered setting the beer onto a built shelf running the length of one side "I hate adventures." He picked up a section of dirty old rope and kicked at a deflated rubber raft. The place smelled more of mold than lake.

"Home for now," Quinn sighed.

"I'm sorry," Evan said. "I should've checked. I should have fucking checked."

The tone said the kid meant it but then he always had been softer than the rest of them.

"You couldn't have known," Quinn said. "You've only had Peggy for a while."

"It's one day not planned," Jason said. "Maybe when we get out there will be a BBQ and another party we can raid."

"Anyone got a deck of cards?"

"I spy with my little—"

Quinn picked up a piece of rubber and threw it at Jason.

"Shut up," he laughed, not that he felt much humor

They found positions to sleep the day away. Jason lay straight out from the wall. Quinn, up against the edge. Evan near the back. Mere feet separated them.

"Quinn," Evan said.

"Go to sleep. You'll drive yourself crazy counting minutes."

"Quinn," Evan said, his voice hitched. Quinn looked up from his place on the floor and saw Evan pale faced. He stared at the door.

Quinn followed Evan's gaze and saw the pink sunrise poking in a couple dozen breaks in the shed walls. Quinn rolled, coming up to a kneeling position.

"Jason," Quinn said.

"What do you want me to do about it?"

The still dim light shimmered in, thinking it was a welcome guest. Quinn looked up. A portion of the roof was gone.

Their bad day just took one step into really bad.

Quinn knew what sun and vampire could really mean. He had seen it in his past, far more graphic than they ever spoke of. His gaze jumped to Evan, the innocent who hadn't done anything to warrant the fate. Quinn's gaze shifted and he found Jason staring at him. Jason raised his eyebrows and shrugged.

Staring at the roof, Quinn took off his denim, ripping it in two, then four. He tossed one piece to Evan.

He heard Jason do the same with his wind breaker and T-shirt, leaving Jason wearing his Celtic cross and jeans.

"Plug something that looks bad." Quinn pulled his shirt off over his head.

He moved to the largest hole while knowing it was that hole in the roof that would cause the most trouble.

Shirtless now, Jason shifted to the shelf hanging waist level, running the length of the room. Putting the five-pack on the floor, it didn't look like it took any effort to pull the wood from the wall. The plank was three feet by eight. Jason carried it to the other side.

"Get in the corner," he said to Evan.

"What?"

"Get in the damn corner."

Jason checked for sharp edges and pulled some rusty nails away. He grabbed the sides and moved it with ease toward Evan.

"What about you two?" Evan sank into the corner.

"We're shifty," Jason smiled.

He placed the shield over the sitting kid, then looked at Quinn.

"Is it going to work?" Quinn mouthed.

Jason nodded. "Should."

Quinn wasn't feeling too much hope in their situation.

"Now what?" Jason asked.

Quinn looked around. More light from big and small holes peeked through. "I guess we dance."

The door was open a foot, but Stuart knocked anyway.

"Enter," Travis grunted.

The stereo held a stack of records, the sound turned low as not to interrupt.

Stuart hated to be the interruption.

Travis had a final tomorrow and biology wasn't his best subject.

"What?" Travis asked.

"They didn't come home."

It took a half second for the head to come up, the pencil to go down and Travis to turn in his chair to face Stuart.

"What the hell does that mean?"

"They're not here. They didn't come back last night."

Stuart checked his watch at the same time Travis checked his.

Travis dropped his arm and looked at the covered window. "It's after noon."

"I'm aware," Stuart said.

Travis stared at Stuart straight on. "They went to the lake. That party."

"It was supposed to go all night," Stuart said, "I assumed they knew to be back before dawn."

Travis stood up and walked to the window. Tension hit his shoulders.

"We're stuck until dark," Travis said.

"I'm aware of that, too," Stuart said.

"Did they say anything to you?" Travis asked.

"Not more than drinking, partying and picking up girls."

Travis put his hand on his forehead and Stuart saw the biology exam losing importance.

"There is nothing we can do for a couple of hours," Stuart said. "You finish in here."

"It's like living with a bunch of baby monkeys," Travis snapped. "We let them loose and they wreak havoc on local ecosystems."

"Hey Jason," Quinn said from four feet away.

His partner in crime answered. "Still here." Hands in his pockets, relaxed in a way only Jason could achieve.

"What's with the redhead?" Quinn asked. "You don't do redheads."

"I didn't say I did a redhead now."

Quinn smiled and nodded with pursed lips. "That is true. I assumed from past experience."

"She was a good girl," Jason smiled. "We only played a little."

"You don't do redheads," Quinn repeated.

Girl questions were generally off limits.

But Quinn knew Jason wasn't going to bitch.

"I found myself in the mood," Jason said.

"You haven't been in the mood for a redhead since 1947."

"Why is that?" Evan asked from his corner, still behind his shield.

"I don't like their pension plan."

Quinn knew what Jason meant. He had been turned by a sexy redhead. Quinn didn't explain it to Evan.

"They don't taste good," Jason said, eyeing the ceiling as he neared an open spot.

"Bullshit," Quinn laughed. "You always said they taste like strawberries."

He heard Evan sigh. "I've never dated a redhead."

"That's because you've never dated," Jason smirked.

"I don't know, Jason," Quinn said. "He had that blonde and brunette practically eating out of his hand on that dance floor."

Jason smiled. "Ahhh, he's growing up…"

He dramatically waved his arms, miscalculating the time. He bit off a curse word when he got burned, his face screwed tight. It was enough to tell Quinn it was worse than Jason let on.

"You okay?" Evan asked.

Jason smiled tight. "Peachy."

"It's 12:15," Evan said from behind the board. "I can take a turn out there."

"Evan, you couldn't even get to one of the spots without going up in smoke."

Quinn reached over without incident to grab one, two, three beers. "Evan, peek out."

His face came out on the side furthest from light. "Catch," Quinn said. He rolled one of the bottles across the uneven floor. The beer bottle made it to its mark.

"We are very short on beverages so make this one last."

No one complained about being cramped. No one complained about being hungry. No one even mentioned missing a dose of *Ace in the Hole*. Quinn figured they would be okay for one day.

Jason caught his beer and twisted the cap. "Warm beer," he said, taking a chug. "Day just keeps getting better."

"You think they noticed yet?"

"Of course they noticed," Jason said. "Question is—did they already rent out our rooms?"

On the city streets, Travis sped a good ten above the speed limit. Once he made the turn past the broken wooden gate onto the dirt road, he hit the high beams then upped the gas.

"I was thinking," Stuart said.

"Why?" Travis asked, without breaking a smile. It was dark outside now. He was driving at a high speed.

"About where we're going to move next."

"We don't move for four years. Why the hell are you thinking of shit like that when we don't move for four years?"

"I miss the Bay," Stuart said. "A lot. It was a great place to live."

Travis risked a glance in Stuart's direction. "Alcatraz was still open. We could get a group rate."

Stuart felt his smile but it felt sad. Losing people sucked. The fear in his gut hurt with the knowledge he might lose more.

"I remember it ending badly," Travis said.

Stuart looked at him. "Quick exit but we brought company. You think it's bad? What we have?"

Travis pursed his lips and didn't answer.

"We got Quinn."

"Walter almost got us," Travis said.

"Almost," Stuart said, trying to keep an optimistic attitude.

He liked Quinn. He liked Evan. If pressed, he might even admit to liking that son-of-a-bitch Irishman. The five of them had something. Unconventional, but real. The knot in his gut seized a little.

They passed a sign proclaiming five miles more.

But they didn't need the miles.

Three shirtless figures appeared on the left side of the dirt road, walking in the dark, their way marked by moonlight.

Travis skidded to a halt, lifting dirt into the air.

The three jumped out of the way as Travis slammed the car into park and came out, his tall frame clearing the low roof.

A curse.

A cheer.

A sigh.

"Where the hell have you been?" Travis snapped.

"Don't even start," Jason said.

"Where's the car?"

Stuart reached into the backseat, grabbing three thermoses of water to hand off.

"Peggy," Evan said. "I didn't get to the tires and spare, yet."

"You had a flat?" Stuart asked. "All this was because of a flat?"

"We had a flat," Quinn confirmed, before downing half the water.

"There was a shack nearby. Not a good one but it looks like it worked," Jason said.

"Damage?" Travis asked.

"Car needs its tire fixed."

"Couple sunburns," Quinn added. "Nothing major."

"You're all okay?" Travis asked.

"Why? Miss us?" Jason smiled.

Stuart smiled back with an equal amount of sarcasm. "Enough to bring a broom, dust pan and three plastic bags."

"What?" Evan gasped.

"They're in the trunk," Travis said. "Figured we'd find a nice bush somewhere out of the way."

Quinn, Jason and Evan stared.

Stuart stuck his hands in his pockets and turned to Travis. "I picked out the bush."

"What bush?" Jason asked on a chuckle.

"The thorn bush in the back that won't behave no matter how many times we beat the shit out of it with shovels when it causes us grief."

Skin Deep
1981

"We'll be there," Travis said before hanging up the phone in the den.

"It's set?" Stuart asked him.

Travis nodded slowly. "Everyone pulled their days at work so we can do this. We leave tonight."

Boise to New Orleans, traveling by car only at night and hanging out in hotels during the day.

It took longer to make the journey this way, but they arrived safely, Jason's SUV locked behind a gate in the French Quarter.

The house set on the same land claimed two centuries ago. Brick with the look of moisture and faded red. The wild plants mixed with the added to climb the outside walls. The bottom floor windows were almost covered.

An hour later they were settled in. Travis sat in his old chair out back, while the others found places to get comfortable.

Nanette—no last name—sat at the white ornate table in her private garden. Water trickled in the fountain centerpiece; a fireplace glowed, providing heat in the dark March night.

She was the kindest person Travis had ever met, though, she never explained her decisions or motives to take him under her care. She was as dangerous as she was beautiful. Her dark skin rich and her black hair to her waist, kept in rolls.

"You did what I wanted you to do, my Tall Man," Nanette smiled. "You became the person you were, then helped others join you."

"I hate their fucking guts and they drive me insane," he said, taking a sip off his brandy and a puff from the expensive cigar she provided.

She laughed. "And you bring them here for protection, why?"

"Because it hurts like a bitch, takes weeks to get through and you will tie them all down one by one and I get to hear them scream."

Jason stretched out his legs and took a drink of his fortified Hurricane.

"So," he pointed between Travis and Nanette. "Did you two ever..." he wiggled his eyebrows and grinned.

"Make stupid faces and look like an ass?" Travis asked.

"Stupid faces might be involved." Jason cocked his head.

Travis glanced at him, tilted his chin to the side. "She kissed me once. About four feet from where you're sitting."

He tried not to smile when Jason's gaze darted to the side.

"And it was really awful." Travis chuckled.

"It was like kissing my brother," she said, shuddering.

The mixture of laughter came in different tones, all sincere.

"I gave him his room. I kept mine."

"In this house?" Evan asked. "This is the same house you've always had?"

She nodded. "Third floor. Once it was his, no one ever slept there but him. I would not allow it. He didn't stay often, but when he did, he needed it and he had it clean."

"That's the room you're in now," Quinn said.

Travis nodded and toasted with his glass.

"He came to the city in 1946," Nanette. "His soul was stronger than the rest. Pure. You could feel an innocence in it that wanted to be rescued. I listened to him for years before his pain became too great for me to bear."

Stuart pointed at Travis. "Him? You're talking about him?" He laughed and leaned back. "Not a side I've seen."

"You saw that side in San Francisco. The night you went for him. You saw him in the street."

"He was a drunk asshole staggering at two in the morning and I was hungry."

"I'm still willing to debate that one," Travis said.

Stuart smiled. "He tasted like shit."

"Fuck you," Travis laughed with the others.

"She came into the Dragon's Bridge," Travis said, "years before Stuart. Place was wild that night. Almost all of them vampires, and those that weren't, didn't care. She walked in and walked me right out the door."

Evan laughed. "You never told me that."

Travis shrugged. "I was like her new toy. She liked me. She taught me the idea of blood-free before I ever thought of it myself. She said I had the soul for it. Took me ten years and a fucking Scotsman to figure out she was right."

"Nanette?" Evan asked timidly. He was on his second Hand Greneade. He took a drink.

"Yes, child?"

"You can do things? I mean, he never really told us but it sounded like you can do things other people can't. Is that true?"

"What are you looking for?" Quinn asked.

Evan looked at him. "Maybe she can change us."

"That's the plan," Stuart said.

"I don't mean tattoos." Evan looked at her. "Can you make us human again?"

Travis saw every one of them sit up and change expressions from hope to excitement to doubt.

"Is that possible?" Jason asked, without his usual humor.

She looked at Evan. "I have everything ready for tomorrow to make it possible to be in the world a little bit easier. It won't be another life, but a brush stroke of color added to your dark world."

"That's not what he asked," Travis pointed out.

"You can, can't you?" Evan asked.

"And what would you do if I said yes, little one? Your family is gone. They moved far away after you were taken."

"Jason can find them."

"How would you explain being alive after missing? What excuse would you give them for making them worry? How would you explain your age?"

Evan stared at the ground, his eyes shifting right and left.

"You miss them," she said. "Everyone here, even me, misses someone."

"Hey, brat?" Jason said.

Evan looked at him. "What would you do, Jason?"

Jason sighed hard. I'm where I'm supposed be, Evan. I might not like it sometimes and I really don't like that no one gave me a choice but this is how it turned out."

"You go taking off for Seattle," Quinn said, "and the taco recipe goes with you. What the hell are we supposed to do?"

"Chocolate pudding cake," Jason said, pointing at Quinn. "Have you ever had a better chocolate pudding cake?"

Evan dropped his chin. "I watched my Mom. She used to make it for birthdays."

Jason got out of the chair, left his drink and moved to the ground beside Evan. He mirrored Evan's position—knees drawn, arms straight, wrists on knees. He looked at the kid, their shoulders touching.

"We can't give you back what they took, but you're one of us. Twisted, and maniacal…"

Travis smiled when Evan did.

"Perverted," Quinn added.

"Abnormal," Stuart said.

"You take off," Jason said, "and we will hunt you down and tie you to the mattress so you can't escape."

Evan looked at him. "You wouldn't do it? Grab the chance to be normal again?"

"Define normal," Quinn said.

"No, Evan," Jason said. "I wouldn't do it. It was too hard to get where we are now. I wouldn't even know how to go back."

Evan looked at Quinn who shook his head. Stuart? The same. It came around to Travis who smiled.

"I wouldn't mind kicking the ass of the guy who did it to me."

"You've done that," Stuart said, deadpan. "Twice."

Travis grinned at him. "Never gets old."

Evan slugged the grinning Jason. "You guys would be lost without me."

"Only reason we make it," Quinn chuckled.

Nanette smiled. "I couldn't do it, little one, even if you wanted. Some powers are beyond me. I have only done the tattoos a handful of times."

"And you are doing them now," Travis said. "We appreciate it."

"Did you tell them what is involved?"

"Pain and suffering?" Jason supplied.

"There is that," Nanette said. "And silence. You will not be able to make a sound. And you will want to."

Travis saw Jason look at Stuart and Stuart look at Quinn.

"We will start in one week and work through the days. Each of you will take a turn during daylight hours oldest to youngest, each layer applied in ink, color and spell. You will not question my methods or techniques."

"Why a week?" Quinn asked.

"I need the time to watch and learn and find your personality. Your mark will carry your inner strengths."

"I know I spent the night in a holey shack with these two recently," Quinn pointed out.

"Shack was barely standing," Jason said, "let alone offering protection."

"Only one of us could hide at a time," Evan said. "The other two had to stand and move with the shadows."

"And those two," Travis said, pointing at Quinn and Jason, "made him hide the whole time."

"Fuck you," Jason laughed. "That fucking brat wouldn't stop whining."

Quinn nodded. "Only way to get him to shut up was to hogtie him with our belts and throw him in that corner."

A wide smile split Evan's face. "Yeah, that's exactly how I remember it. You looked pretty with your pants falling down."

Stuart's design screamed Celtic.

Quinn's medical.

Jason's was the only one with color and he would never be able to deny his Irish roots.

Evan stared at his design on the paper on the table in the dining room, the others stood beside him. Travis saw him lift the paper up to get a closer look. The Count from Sesame Street was drawn in thick strokes, numbers curved above The Count's head.

His gaze came up to Travis.

He pointed to the others. "How come theirs are so boring?"

Stuart walked into the room first.

He was about to be tied down, Travis knew.

The 18th century table, upholstered in red timber and fabric, had leather straps on the sides to hold, but straining them didn't ease the pain.

The room was subdued with soft light by candle, the smell of wax but the events that occurred within those four walls was the stuff nightmares were made of.

There were no numbing agents. No tattoo gun like the shop half a mile away. A multi-layer process with layer upon layer added with each personalized design.

Two hours later, Stuart came out of the room in a white muscle shirt, pale and shaky. His hand below the pink skin on his right bicep.

"Brass needle and ink?"

"It's not ink." Travis said, handing Stuart a glass of ice water.

"I figured that out by the smell." He drank the water down by half.

"Did Quinn go in?" Travis asked.

Stuart nodded and put the glass on the table.

"You sure this is worth it? A lot of time, and too much pain."

Travis gave no judgment on Stuart's inability to hold up. They weren't just taking on that shit she called ink. She was putting in spells that would combine to protect all of them.

"Do me a favor," Stuart asked, putting his head on his folded arms on the table.

"What?"

"Tell the Irishman I beat his ass."

Travis locked his gaze with Jason's, who stood silently just that side of the door.

"You were a rock," Travis said.

Jason raised his gaze, smiled and nodded, then walked away.

Ten days later, Jason was the last one to join them in the back garden at two o'clock in the afternoon, the sun high. Chicory coffee was served with beignets, homemade and sweet.

"How long can we stay out here?" Quinn asked Nanette.

"It will depend. Each one of you will react differently. The clouds will help. Direct sun will still burn but filtered daylight will be safe. You will each find your own place."

Evan looked at his arm then up at the sky. "I don't even feel the sun There's no burn."

"Then have two beignets," she smiled. "And I will tell you about our next adventure."

Wrong Place, Wrong Time
1982

Travis had worked at The Crab House as a waiter for three out of five years the five of them had been in San Francisco. Never late for a night of serving, he was easy to find when you needed him. To date, not a lot of people came looking for him.

Jason's mind could not set on any one point. Everything in his head bounced around with no direction.

He pulled his collar tight on his denim coat to ward off the moist chill. People moved around but he shut out their noise.

He remembered the movie he had seen had started at 9:50pm. It had to be after midnight now.

He bumped into a line backer's shoulder, uttering an 'excuse me,' as he walked on.

There were so many people on the street, he thought. Different faces, different colors of coats. It was late, he thought. They should be home. Jason could hear them all. Their breathing, their heartbeats in their chests. These were sounds he left behind over a decade ago. Once prominent with his lifestyle, they had faded as he transcended from vampire sense to not having that acute sense.

Tonight they came back in Technicolor detail.

Sweaty, his breath short, his hands shaking in his pockets, he got to the restaurant. Pulling back the glass door, he stepped in to scan the room.

There was no Travis.

Jason's last hope sank.

The waitress, Monica, pointed toward the back.

"He's on a break, Jason." She came a little closer. He took a step back.

She stopped walking toward him.

"Are you feeling alright?"

That was genuine concern he saw in her features, but he didn't trust himself to get too close.

"Caught a cold." He managed to smile and make it look real.

"Garlic with honey," she said. "That's what my Granma always said."

He nodded and kept the smile in place. "Thanks. I'll try that."

Jason retraced his steps out the front door and turned up the alley to the south.

He saw Alcatraz out of the corner of his eye, thinking it looked like nice housing. No one was out there. Everyone would be safe.

The dark alley smelled of the nearby bay gone bad. You could feel the memories of people who did things he didn't want to think about.

Travis' cigarette heralded his presence before Jason actually reached him. Travis was the last to hold out when all of them had given up the habit over the years.

Glen Mason, a waiter who not only worked beside Travis but laughed at Travis' stupid jokes was standing with him. Travis, taller by a foot than Glen, was easy to spot from a distance. He leaned back against the building and drew the end of the smoke to a bright orange glow. The yellow light bulb above him glowed dim under the grime.

Travis' back went straight. His arm dropped, the glow of the cigarette falling with his hand.

"What are you doing here?"

"I need to talk to you," Jason said. "It couldn't wait."

"I get off at two."

Jason stared, but didn't answer.

Travis looked down the alley, behind Jason. "Where's your car?"

Jason shook his head at Travis. "I don't know. I don't know where I left it."

Glen coughed and dropped his cigarette on the ground, crushing it with his toe.

"I'll see you inside," he said to Travis. Travis absently nodded.

"You lost your car? Pretty sure you kind of liked it."

Jason came forward and Travis' head fell back. Jason stopped at the look on Travis' face.

"Is there a reason you smell like fresh blood?"

Jason looked at him, his voice breathless and hushed. "I don't know. I don't know what happened. I got sick and lost the car and walked here."

"You took a victim?"

Jason looked at him, his throat freezing. "I don't know. Maybe. I think so. Maybe."

Travis' came off the wall and stepped forward. "Where?"

"I don't know," Jason said. "He was there, Travis and then it was over. I don't have a clue what happened in between."

Travis grabbed Jason by the upper arm and moved down the alley.

They got to his Pontiac Trans Am, making the trip home in record time.

Jason sat in the living room in an upholstered chair, his hands clasped out in front of him, his head bowed. He leaned forward, still feeling sick from the feast, still wishing he would remember more details of what had happened.

"Is he dead?" Stuart asked.

Jason looked up and rolled his tongue in his mouth. "I think so," he said. "He was on the ground. He wasn't moving and I didn't do a hell of a lot of checking."

"Were you seen?" Quinn asked. "Was anyone around?"

"I was in the back parking lot, behind the theater. It's small. Only a couple cars can fit, maybe six or seven. I didn't see anyone else around."

"But this kid?" Quinn asked.

Jason nodded, remembering more than he had. "Yeah. He was there when I got out of the movie. I came up the alley and he sorta appeared and followed me. Yeah, I remember that. He was real high. That was obvious."

"And it's okay?" Evan asked. "To take a druggie?"

"No," Jason snapped. "It wasn't okay. I don't know what happened. I wasn't having cravings, I wasn't even hungry. I had just eaten a pound of M&M's, for Christ's sake."

"What was the movie?" Travis asked.

"Blade Runner."

"Anything about it stick out? Any scenes? Was there blood and guts in it?"

"It was a good movie?" Jason suggested. "'Cuz yes, there was blood and guts but I don't remember any of it setting anything off. I didn't walk out of the theater with a plan to take a victim."

"Maybe something else set you off? Because we have to figure out what set you off."

"It was a sci fi. A good one. Harrison Ford, Rutger Haur. There wasn't anything that would take me there."

"You're sure?"

Elbows on his knees, he braced his hands and stopped trying so hard to remember.

"Pretty sure."

Jason leaned back and sighed. Talking calmly, talking it through once again, more came up as time distanced itself from the event.

Quinn came close, holding his wrist toward Jason.

Jason looked at the slice that hadn't been there a minute ago. Quinn's pearl handled switch blade was in his other hand, a thin layer of blood on it.

"What the fuck are you doing?" Travis said abruptly.

"Close your eyes," Quinn told Jason. "Smell."

"That's bullshit," Jason snapped, pulling away.

"Close your eyes," Quinn said again in his doctor/patient voice.

And Jason trusted Quinn.

Doubting it would work, Jason paused before leaning a little forward.

"You almost never get this, right? But you smelled it tonight, right? You more than smelled it."

"It made me sick," Jason said. "Violently. I had to pull over three times coming home."

He opened his eyes and looked at Quinn. "That's how I lost the car. I went to a bush then walked."

"You were in the movie? Did you stay for the credits?"

"No, I left right away. Walked to the car—"

He stopped talking and stared at the floor, remembering more.

"He was in the alley," Jason said. "He followed me to my car." Jason chuckled. "He was high and he was funny and he wouldn't leave me alone."

Quinn stepped back as Evan brought a rag.

Jason looked up and stared at Travis. "He wanted money so I gave him a five and he wanted more."

"What did he do?" Travis asked.

"I tried to get to the car door and he grabbed me. And then I'm holding him and he's dead and I'm bloody and I don't have a fucking clue what happened."

"Anything ever happen like this before?" Travis asked, standing, his arms crossed.

"I wouldn't hide this. I don't want to do this. I went to you to figure it out."

"I know you did," Travis said. "And you did good."

"I'm following the program. I haven't varied it. I never looked at anyone before. Are you going to make me move out? I don't want to move out."

"No," Travis said, quick, easing at least one fear.

Jason looked around and saw agreement in all their expression.

He sighed hard and dropped his gaze to the floor, then back up.

They had faced a lot of bullshit over the years. When one of them was in trouble for something, the others played back-up.

"What do you think happened?" Travis asked Quinn.

Quinn looked at him. "It's hard to say. We're all basically walking experiments. Nothing we have done has been done before."

"But we've been doing it for years," Stuart said.

"Yeah," Quinn said. "With all of us having pretty much the same results. But the three of us all started at the same time, at least close. Evan and Jason were later."

"Am I going to do this?" Evan asked.

"No," Stuart said, soft.

Quinn shrugged. He walked over to the floor lamp beside Jason, snapped it on and tilted the shade to put the full glare of light in Jason's eyes.

"What the fuck?" Jason snapped, covering his eyes with his palm.

"How long have you been light sensitive?"

"I didn't know I was," he said, still covering his eyes.

"And restless. Your leg is bouncing about a mile a minute."

Jason dropped his hand and looked at his leg, stopping it at once.

Quinn turned the light off. "You can't sleep. And when you do, you have nightmares."

"How did you know that?"

"I've seen it before. Drug addicts treated in the ER. It's a sign of withdrawal. And I'm not saying I know that's what is happening here, but it's a place to start."

"To my knowledge," Travis said. "Jason doesn't take drugs. And if he did, the amount he would need to get stoned isn't in the state."

"We're all addicts, Travis," Quinn said. "I don't care what you want to call it. We had our drug of choice, unconventional, of course, but easy to obtain at low cost." Travis glared back. Jason looked between the two of them.

"Which theater," Travis asked.

"Market Street."

"And you were heading home?"

"Started that way. I wanted to get back here. But like I said, I got sick a couple of times and had to pull over. I guess I just got out and walked."

"Sick, lost car, doesn't remember," Travis said to Quinn.

"Sick because his was rejecting what he got. That's not a bad thing. If the mind wanted but the body rejected, we have hope. He's not totally screwed yet."

"Sitting right beside you," Jason moaned. "Can hear every word."

Quinn ignored him. "Car, I don't know. He might not have known. Not remembering where it is? It's what he'd do, for the traumatic ones. He wouldn't remember. I know of two others before he came to us. The more it hurt him, the less he'd remember."

"Why?" Jason asked.

"Because your mind can't handle the memory or the guilt. Your brain tried to shut it out."

"What two?" Travis asked.

Quinn shook his head. "Not for me to give them up and it won't help here. If he wants to tell you, then wait. The car has to be somewhere between the theater and here. Two of you go for it using the most common route he would take. It's out there. And we need it tonight, before it's towed. There might be evidence on it and it's registered in his name. I'll put him to bed and under guard, while I figure this out."

"I'll stay in the room with him," Stuart said.

"Would you all stop talking about me while I am right here?"

"If he turns violent? Do you have a plan?" Travis asked.

"I do," Stuart said.

"What the fuck are you planning on doing?" Jason snapped.

Stuart smiled. "Beating you senseless then tying you up with duct tape and rope until Quinn figures it out."

Jason sat back in the chair, a hand on each knee, his shoulders slumped. "I thought—"

"I know what you thought," Stuart said. "But we don't do that to our own. We'll get through this."

Jason didn't leave his room. Bathroom breaks were allowed with someone always on guard. Meals were given to him at his desk.

This was partially due to them wanting to make sure he didn't get away from them.

And partially due to him, not wanting to get away from them.

His hands shook all the time, his gut pounding like it owned a sledge hammer. He was scared. Scared of what he might be capable of doing and to whom.

One of the others was with him the majority of the time, taking shifts. Travis took the most shifts since he had nowhere to be at night after losing his job. The Crab House loved his work, and even though he had never missed a day, they were not forgiving him about walking off from a shift, even for a family emergency. He never said anything, but Jason felt bad.

Quinn came in and handed him a tall plastic blue glass.

"What is it?" Jason asked looking at the liquid.

"I played with the formula, double timed the concentration of everything, and added some new. It should work."

Jason put the glass to his nose. "Doesn't smell too bad."

"Majority of the stuff I did, might make it better."

Jason looked at it, then up to Quinn. "Really? Cuz I don't think I ever mentioned how shit-like the last batch was."

"You told me almost every day."

"Really?" Jason grinned. "I'm having memory problems."

"Fuck you," Quinn smiled.

"You just might do that." Jason raised the glass in toast. "To our brilliant doctor. May he know what the fuck he is doing." Jason drank the whole glass.

"That's not nearly as bad."

"Glad you like it," Quinn said. "We're going to try you on two glasses a day and I want you to start hitting the gym harder. Get that going. We're all doing the same, at least for a while. We're going to keep the new formula."

Jason stared at him.

"If it can happen to you, it can happen to any of us. We just have different metabolisms. Yours adapted quicker. I think. I'm pretty sure that's what happened, but I don't have any test cases to check. We do this, Jason and I think you're going to be okay."

His name was Dwayne Simmons.

He was nineteen years old and a known multi choice drug user, financing his habits with theft and prostitution.

He had two younger sisters in Modesto he hadn't seen in four years. His parents, though devastated at their loss were not surprised.

Jason stared at his yellow legal pad. He tried not to think of the blue eyes, blonde hair and easy laugh. Calls to the PD. Calls to the coroner's office. Calls to the places Jason was able to track.

Everyone liked Dwayne.

Cause of death had not been the expected drug overdose, Jason found from a Modesto newspaper. Exsanguination. He had been drained of blood with marks on his neck.

The coroner leaned toward animal attack, but no animals had been found near the scene. No other victims had been reported. His body had been found in a back lot, in the dark, eight hours after he had died.

But Jason needed to do more. He had the maps out, the route planned. If he left right at sunset, he could make it in one of the guys' car. He could get to Green Woods Cemetery in Modesto.

And maybe make a difference.

"How is that going to help?" Travis asked from the door, catching Jason unaware.

"I could see him," Jason said. "Maybe say something."

"How much did you get for the Porsche at that used lot?"

Jason glanced up at him. The new formula was working. The jitters were gone, the nightmares were gone as well. He slept undisturbed during the day, as long as he didn't think of Dwayne.

"If you wanted to give it away for that cheap, all of us liked it. We could have worked something out."

"I didn't want it here," Jason said. "I looked at it and saw him and it smelled like that night."

"Jason, there is nothing in that grave but a shell. You know that. You can take the drive and try to beat the sun, but it's not going to change anything. It won't make it not have happened."

"I couldn't even call his parents. I was afraid it might hurt them."

Travis walked in and stood over Jason and his desk. Jason didn't look up.

"So, use that over-developed, annoying-as-hell brain you have and figure out how to make the loss of someone who didn't want to save himself into something that matters."

The world kept moving along even without Dwayne Simmons. It was something Jason had to face every night when he got up. Finding a way to make it matter was his passion.

Alone at two in the morning, Jason parked illegally in front of the building, leaned against his Corvette and crossed his arms.

The light on the sign of the former warehouse shined bright against the dimly lit street.

The Dwayne Simmons Rehabilitation Center, open just eighteen hours had people already registered in various programs. The staff that Jason had picked from a distance, were the best, willing to stand by their charges.

Opened this morning, it was three years to the day after the death of Dwayne Simmons, financed by the development of several video games and sold to the arcade industry. All trademarks were held by the foundation in front of him.

Jason planned the opening. He didn't attend it.

He heard Travis' car engine sound as it pulled up behind him.

Two doors shut. Jason looked. Travis leaned against the door, his hands in his pockets. Stuart to the right, on the other side of the car.

No one said a word and later Quinn walked up with Evan.

A few minutes passed before anyone spoke.

"You thought you could keep this quiet?" Evan asked.

"Hoped."

Evan chuckled. "Moron."

Jason stood in the dark, the moist air full of salt and wondered how he had ever gotten along without them.

"You're all fucking assholes," he said.

Quinn laughed beside him.

"Does it appease the guilt?" Travis asked without looking at him.

"Nope," Jason said. "I still did something I shouldn't have done."

"But you did something good, Irishman," Stuart said in his Scottish accent. "You took a tragedy, and pulled out something good."

Compliments from Stuart to Jason didn't happen very often. Jason smiled and thought maybe, he shouldn't have replaced Stuart's deodorant with cream cheese last night.

"Come on," Travis said, stepping away from the car. "There is lasagna ready at the house, a couple of bottles of champagne to go with it and some French bread to get into the oven. I might have even picked someone's favorite dessert."

"What did you get?" Jason asked.

"Chocolate torte."

Jason stayed still, smiling behind his pursed lips.

Travis nodded his head to the left.

"Let's go home."

High Jinks
1991

"You wanted to see me, Mr. Ricci?"

Travis pulled his reading glasses off and reached up to rub his eyes. The glasses were for show, but the eyestrain was real. "Can you shut the door, Phil?"

Travis knew the kid was nineteen. Phil shut the door.

Travis rested his elbows on the desk. "I think we're the last ones out."

"Yeah," Phil said, walking toward the desk. "The last group left about ten minutes ago."

"Did they lock up?"

Phil nodded while Travis eyed him.

Phil had worked at The Sugar Oyster a little longer than Travis. The kid hadn't taken offense when the old manager left and Travis stepped in. He had liked the kid, thought he had potential.

"You needed to talk to me?" Phil asked.

Travis looked up at him and motioned to a chair. "The police were here today."

68

"Yeah, I'm sorry. It sucks."

"Your girlfriend, Rhonda," asked, "She's missing?"

Phil nodded. "And they think I had something to do with it. That's just crazy," he sputtered.

Travis leaned back in the chair, folding his hands over his middle. "Where were you this morning, before you came here?"

"What?"

Travis shrugged one shoulder. "I'm curious. You came in late and had to change your shirt."

"I spilled coffee on it."

"It didn't smell like coffee," Travis said.

Phil's gaze came up. "It was coffee."

"Okay," Travis smiled, letting the silence drag.

Phil huffed out a breath, looking annoyed. "Are you going to fire me? For the police? I don't think they'll be back. There's nothing to find here."

"Why would I do that?"

Phil stood up and started pacing, left to right in front of the desk. "The police were here, everyone's looking at me. I don't know what she does or why."

"I walked around here this morning," Travis said casually. "Trying to figure out what the hell that smell was. I asked, no one else could smell it, which was too bad."

"What are you talking about?"

"The dead, Phil. The dead have a scent all their own and today, you were walking around wearing it."

"What?" He smelled his arm. "I don't smell anything."

"So Rhonda's dead, that's a safe bet. You did it or you know who did and you were around the body before you came here today."

Phil puffed out his chest. "What the hell are you talking about? It's her high jinks. That's what she called them, you know. When she pulled her little stunts to make people look. She was a pain in the ass to deal with, now…"

"Past tense?"

Phil stared at him.

"You're talking about Rhonda in the past tense. Where is she?"

"I don't know." Phil whined. "But I'm meeting some friends. I have to get going. Is that all you wanted to ask me because I have to get going."

"Look at me," Travis said.

Suggestion, a tool for hunting that Travis had put behind him with a promise to himself never to use on a human again. He thought of Rhonda, her smiling face. Travis hadn't met her much but she had everything going for her–school, grades—it was tragic she hooked up with a loser like Phil. Even Travis, who had been around murderers for decades, hadn't realized this kid was capable of taking that way out.

He had Phil's stare and held it. He never really knew what gave them the ability to control thoughts when they turned, but it was something he knew how to manipulate.

"Where's Rhonda?"

Phil tried not to stare back. He tried to keep quiet. The struggle was enough to break out sweat on his forehead.

70

When he spoke, his voice sounded hollow and breathless. He stuttered. "I moved her…this morning…before coming here."

"Where?"

"About forty-five miles outside of town."

"Could you find her again?"

Phil's nod jerked his head. "Yeah. No problem."

The *why* crept into Travis mind, but he didn't think it really mattered. Phil was alive and Rhonda was dead.

"I couldn't do it," Phil said. "Not with her and a baby. Rhonda wouldn't get rid of it. What the hell was I supposed to do?"

Travis stared at him, his teeth grinding. The fury he controlled still sent sparks up his arms to his shoulders. He considered the vampire laws against what this kid had done. Travis had the means to bring justice to a girl who deserved better. Except, Phil being dead would not bring peace to Rhonda's folks.

Travis gritted his teeth and picked up the phone.

He stared at the kid, glaring. "Sit in that chair."

Phil looked at it then back to Travis. He took the seat.

"You're tied up, do you get that?"

Phil struggled against bonds only he could see. "Come on," he whined. "Let me go. It's not that big of a deal."

"You can't move."

Phil froze, his whines becoming pathetic.

Travis dialed.

911.

"I have a kid here in the back room of The Sugar Oyster. His name is Phil Nesmeth. He just confessed to the murder of Rhonda James. He knows where she is."

Travis listened.

"He's not moving. Take your time."

He hung up the phone and tried—though not hard—and to feel something for this kid he had known two years. Disgust was all that came up. Travis got up and came around his desk.

Travis leaned over close, to talk right to Phil's face. "Rhonda was pregnant?" He asked.

"Yes," Phil whined, fear on his wet face.

"And you knew it was yours?"

"That chick? She was too hung up to sleep with anyone else."

Travis took Phil's chin and forced the kid to look straight at him. "That noise that never stops, the one you hear twenty-four hours a day, seven days a week? That's the sound of your child's heartbeat. Do you understand Phil? You will never get that sound out of your head."

Phil looked up at Travis with scared eyes. "Do you hear that?" Phil asked. "What is that? Make it stop."

"It will never stop," Travis said, his hands shook and his breathing hurt. He thought of Rhonda scared, knowing she couldn't stop Phil.

"Make it stop," Phil gasped.

"Live with it, you son-of-a-bitch."

Travis stood straight and watched the kid fight against the sound in his head. He felt no pity for a father who could kill the mom and the unborn child. Travis reached for his black wool coat and gloves and headed out the door...to a bar where he would try to drink this memory away.

Good Night, Sweet Dreams
1994

Walking past the lighted sign that proclaimed *Church of the Rising Son*, Jason Sullivan moved slowly, the cold, starless night having no ill effect on him. Nebraska was kick ass bitter. It had been when he was a kid, it was going to be now in the late fall when funerals seemed most appropriate. His gut ached at everything he had seen tonight, when he knew, in reality, it had gone exactly as it should.

He sat through the funeral in the back pew, surrounded by three generations of people he should have known his whole life. His insides twisted watching his relatives. The pain hit deep and low, putting down roots when he wanted to walk away and leave it behind.

Later, as he moved through the crowd at the reception, he had heard the whispers of "Who is that?" "He looks familiar." "I can't place him."

"Excuse me," a small voice said.

A girl about eight with brown hair and green eyes stared up at him.

"Did you know Nancy?" she asked.

He nodded and smiled. "A long time ago."

"She was teaching me to make a pie. Sometimes we made a cherry. Sometimes apple."

He grinned at the sadness. "Boysenberry was her favorite," he said.

The little girl smiled back before being hushed by what had to be her Mom.

Jason bolted before the conversation could start.

Hours later, most people having headed home with the drop in temperature, Jason wandered up the path with his hands in his trouser pockets, the black suit with black shirt and black tie.

He couldn't hear the muffled sounds of people talking or soft music from the hall. He figured that meant he was alone. He went to the side entrance of the building and popped the flimsy lock. Ignoring the light switch, he moved to the back of the church for one of the folding chairs, carrying it down the aisle to the front, setting it directly beside the coffin.

A three-foot photo of Nancy's aged and smiling face watched him. There were more flower arrangements than he could count, filling the entire church with the scent of spring on this November night.

Jason knew the face in the photo, had known it his whole life. Nancy and he had been the spitting image of each other, sharing not only every feature but the greenest of green eyes on earth. He looked at the colored photo and even in the dark he could see hers had never faded.

He reached in his back pocket to get his wallet and pulled out the cracked black and white photo he always carried. He ran his finger over Nancy at fifteen. She was standing next to him, their arms around each other just one day before he boarded the bus that took him back east.

Every part of being turned had sucked like nothing could possibly suck but losing her hurt more than just about anything…except the knowledge she had lost him without the slightest warning.

She never got an answer. She never had any closure. And he had done that to her. He closed his eyes, and now in a life full of guilt, he felt that one the most.

The overhead light went on. His eyes squinted, his breath caught. There was an old man standing in the corner of the room, his fingers still on the switch.

"We closed down the building for a reason. You got one for being here?"

Jason put the photo away then slipped his wallet into his pocket. He shook his head. "Not really. Just wasn't fully done saying good-bye."

"There's the graveside service tomorrow morning for that. The broken lock on the door?"

"I won't be able to make that, Father Simon. And I will pay for the lock and door, if there was any damage to it."

"You know me?"

Jason nodded. "Yeah, I used to live around here. Pretty good sermons, if I recall."

"And you are?"

"A friend of Nancy's."

"I know she was popular across the board but you seem a might young to have been hanging around her much. Are you one of her students?"

"Okay," Jason said.

"Not sure about that?" he chuckled.

Jason tried to smile. "I can live with it."

The old man walked into the room with more confidence and spry than a man of his age would, because, man, Jason thought, he had to be way north of ninety. He moved quickly, stopping in front of Jason.

Jason leaned back in the chair, stretched out his legs and put his hands in his pockets.

The old man stood near the foot of the coffin.

"She was much loved," he said, looking at Jason. "Friends with everyone. Her graduated students often stopped her to say she made a difference in their lives."

"That's sweet," Jason smiled.

"She was married to Kevin for forty-three years, until his death and she loved him every day even after."

Jason looked at the floor.

"As I got older," Father Simon said, "it got harder for me to get around and she wasn't exactly a spring chicken."

Jason grinned and almost chuckled.

"She would take me on her trips to Walmart or Sam's Club and help me shop and I swear eight friends would stop her to say 'hi' in the store. She was a remarkable woman whom everyone just loved."

Jason brushed the tears off his face, not even trying to hide them from the minister.

"She was an inspiration," Father Simon said. "Able to hand it out as well as bring it in and she appreciated every ounce of it. Only one thing marred her life and it was something she always carried."

Jason leaned forward in the chair and looked up at the old man.

"When she was fifteen, she lost something she loved more than anything else in this world."

"Life sucks sometimes," Jason said, looking back at the floor.

"She lost her big brother who was more of a big brother to her than other girls get of their big brothers. She adored him. There was this look in her eyes you had to strain to see on most days, but it was always there."

Jason clasped his hands together and stared at Father Simon.

"He was here one minute, expected home for the holidays and then a call came from back east of tragedy and he was just gone. No note. No sign. No phone call afterwards to say he was okay or just delayed someplace. I think that's what she always hoped for but days turned into weeks and the weeks into years and then one day it settled over her like a dark cloud. He was gone and she was never going to know."

"Yeah," Jason said, shifting in his seat. "These life events you don't foresee when you make a single decision that should just be a quick good time. It ends up costing you everything you ever had. They're hard to deal with in your own universe, let alone contemplate what that stupid decision did to the people you leave behind."

"And yet, you're not asking a single question about a mysterious disappearance no one in this town was ever able to explain and let me assure you, enough people tried."

"It's not my business," Jason said. "Her personal life and her private thoughts. I just came to say good-bye."

"Really?" Father Simon said. "I kind of have the feeling what happened with her is more important to you than anyone else. And saying good-bye now might be a little later than she needed."

"Now's the only time I could and since it was the right one considering the circumstances, I don't think I did too bad."

"When you were ten years old," Father Simon said catching Jason's gaze, "you read the Bible cover to cover in one weekend. By the end of the next week you had hit the Book of Common Prayer. For the next month, you checked out every book there was on religion from the library and pulverized them into your over-expanding brain."

Jason looked at the floor and smiled.

"When you were done, you started correcting me in religion class on Sundays."

Jason looked at him.

"You did the same thing at school to your English teachers, your science teachers, your history teachers, your math teachers."

Jason shrugged. "I got bored easy and they were getting all the facts wrong."

"When you boarded that bus, I think we all secretly rejoiced that you were finally gone."

Jason laughed.

"You are Jason Sullivan," he said.

Jason looked at him and thought about the answer. He knew what he was supposed to say but somehow it didn't seem to matter right now.

"You disappeared without a trace in the forties."

"1947," Jason said.

"Your roommate was found dead and you were gone and so everyone assumed those two things had something to do with each other."

"They did," Jason sighed. He brought his gaze up.

"Somebody did something? Which might account for the disappearance but it doesn't explain why you are sitting here, looking just about the same as you did when I last saw you half a century ago."

Jason licked his lips and looked at the large crucifix over the altar. He was raised in this church, had been here so many times he couldn't count. Nancy had been married right where that coffin stood and it was the exact spot where they had both been baptized. According to vampire lore, he shouldn't even be sitting here. But to hell with that, he figured. Almost all the legends were wrong anyway so why not fuck with this one, too.

"When I was twenty-three," he said, "three weeks before Christmas, I was scheduled to come home for the holidays. I was going to hitchhike which sounded tedious, but I was looking forward to it." He sat up in the chair and braced his elbows on his knees. "Man, I was burned out on school. Every day was a struggle to get by with money and I just wanted to go home and see my family and not think about grades and homework and whatever shitty part time job I could get next. But it all changed."

"What do you mean changed?"

"I met a girl who I wasn't planning on knowing for long. She did something. It altered me, not in a good way and so I had to think outside the box."

"You were always good at that, but why not the aging?"

"Part of the package," Jason said. "You know, I am seventy-two years old, trapped in the body of a twenty-three year old and I still get carded when I go to a bar." He looked at Father Simon. "Drives me nuts."

"You're not making a lot of sense, but I have a feeling it's about as much sense as you're going to make."

"Probably."

"Has it been a hard life?"

Jason nodded. "Started out that way. I was alone most of the time. I did some really bad shit that I try never to think of. Hurt a lot of people who didn't deserve to be hurt, never really figured out how to make up for that." He looked again at Father Simon.

"That's severe."

Jason shrugged and nodded. "I had to accept what I lost." He looked at the coffin and the photo. He sighed hard. "I tracked her for years. Even before the Internet. Losing her just about killed me. I knew when she got married, when she had her first kid, a boy she named Jason Patrick that made me proud and sad at the same time than any single event in my life."

"He had a son," Father Simon said. "Named him the same."

Jason smiled at the old man's words.

"When everything changed in 1947, I had already done my Christmas shopping for home which wasn't a hell of a lot since I was broke. Man, I was broke. I was broke like most people can't imagine which is kind of funny now."

"Why is that funny?"

Jason looked at him. "I'm not so broke anymore. Pretty much the contrary and it's kind of nice after so many years of struggling. There was a shop right off the campus with this little silver ring with a turquoise stone in it. I watched in the window for weeks before I even made the attempt to buy it." He closed his eyes and remembered. "It was perfect for her. But, cash was a problem. So I made a deal with the shop owner. I handed over what cash I could and then committed every Saturday for the next year to pay it off. Never even blinked because I knew she would love it."

Jason gazed at Father Simon with unshed tears blurring his view.

"I never reached home," Jason said. "But I mailed the ring from the road within a week of disappearing with a note that I might be late for Christmas. I wanted to make sure she got it. That was the last communication I ever had with my family."

"What was so bad that you couldn't come back?"

Jason's brow rose and he blinked. "I'm twenty-three years old right now when in reality I graduated from MIT in 1945. Do you really think I got into anything good?"

"Jason, she's wearing it right now."

Jason's gaze slid up. "What?"

"She got the ring in the mail. She never took it off, her whole life. I know the family discussed it when it was time and they were getting her ready. Some of them wanted to keep it as an heirloom, but in the end it was decided to keep it with her. She was expecting to meet you in heaven when she got there and she wanted something with her to let you know it was her after she had grown old. No matter how much she always hoped you would walk in the door, she always felt you being there waiting for her was the only logical reason why you would never have contacted her."

Jason felt tears burn his eyes again and some escaped to roll down his cheeks.

"I don't know where my kind goes when they die," he said, "but I doubt it's heaven."

"She never forgot you and she loved you until her dying day. I think you need to know that."

Jason nodded his head and stood. He walked to the coffin and placed his hand on the smooth wood to rub it back and forth. "Sorta felt the same way."

He turned back to Father Simon and took a deep breath before letting it out slowly. There was no use trying to stop the tears. They would probably haunt him in the privacy of his own room for a long, long time. But there was a way to stop any of this from going further.

He walked straight up and looked the minister in the eyes.

"Father Simon, look at me."

The old man brought his faded gaze up to Jason's.

Vampires had too many tricks and some of the tricks that was used for treachery and betrayal could now be used to cover your tracks. Jason spoke very softly and held the gaze firmly. "The lock was broken by vandals. When you came in here, you saw no one. Nancy was laying at peace and you didn't see, hear or speak to anyone. Do you understand?"

Father Simon kind of shook his head, but then he nodded. "No one was here."

Jason put his hands in his pockets and turned to head down the aisle when he stopped and looked at the preacher still standing where he left him. "And thank you. You will remember the thank you."

Jason got to the front doors. He paused to look at the scarred wooden collection box that he had moved on more than one occasion when he had been an altar boy. The letters across the front had never changed: *Tithes and Offerings.*

He reached into his wallet, pulled out one of the fifties, put the wallet away then leaned the bill up against the wall. Pulling the pen from his inside jacket pocket, he used his thick, bold, all cap handwriting to scribble across the currency. *For the broken lock.*

Sliding the pen back, he folded the bill into quarters, tucked it in the slot and turned around one more time to see the church where he had spent every Sunday of his youth, now with a big wooden box at the front surrounded by a thousand flowers and a minister in a chair trying to figure out what had just happened.

Knowing his past was finally over with the loss of the person who mattered most to him, Jason didn't even try to wipe the tears away.

He simply turned, pushed the doors and stepped out into the bitter cold Nebraska night.

Seven Steps

1996

"You have lost someone close?"

Jason sighed, his hands planted flat on the tablecloth. He opened his eyes to stare at her.

Not bad looking. Red hair, though. Her make-up was heavy, the outfit more costume than clothes.

"Yeah," he said.

"A family member," she said. "But not your father. Maybe a mother?" She closed her eyes tighter.

He knew it was bullshit. Every time he visited a new psychic he knew he was not going to find an answer to the engulfing pain that never ended.

He had tried talking to shrinks but that had been a bust, him lying to them about time and dates while they explained the seven stages of grief.

Shock & denial, he got past those two. Pain & guilt, maybe were under control.

It was the anger and bargaining he couldn't quit. No matter how often he screamed to the heavens to send her back, Nancy stayed far away.

Why hadn't he contacted her? Or shown up on her doorstep? Would it really have been so horrible if he had let Nancy known that he was doing okay, given the circumstances? Their relationship would have been unorthodox, but they would have had one.

"You're older than you look," the woman said to him, from across the small table. "It was your lover. You lost a lover. An accident…"

Jason closed his eyes and shook his head. This was bullshit. The whole idea was bullshit. No professional would ever have the answer to fill this gaping hole in his chest.

"That's right," he said. He opened his eyes to stare at his hundred dollar bill on the table. There were sixteen psychics in this town and he planned on going through every single one of them even for no other reason than to have it clarified that it *was* bullshit. "She fell off a stool," he said, "reaching for the spaghetti sauce."

"Yes," the physic smiled. "She says that."

Jason pulled his hands back and covered his face, pressing his fingers into his eye sockets.

"She loved you," Madame Whatever said. Jason dropped his hands to the table and stared at her.

"She loved you very much."

Jason showed the kid the side door exit, then carried the kid's computer to the table next to the others. Fixing the sucker might not pay his bills but it kept him busy.

The guilt never left him, his mind repeating the sonata — his fault, fate wasted.

Why the hell hadn't he made that trip before it was too late?

"Catch," a voice said from behind him.

He turned in time to have the *100 Grand Bar* hit him in the chest. He held it there with a flat palm.

Stuart stood across from him, the red paper pulled down on his own. He chewed slowly.

"What?" Jason snapped because it's what he did these days.

"You looked hungry the last time I saw you."

The accent had always bothered Jason. Right now, it really pissed him off.

He threw the bar back. Stuart caught it.

"Taking chocolate from one of us is a sin now?" Stuart asked.

"What?" Jason snarled.

"You bite all our heads off just about every time we're in the same room. And by the way, you snap at Evan like that again and the rest of us will give up on you."

Mildly confused, Jason stared and didn't speak.

"You don't remember?" Stuart asked. "Last night, he missed some of the trash. You called him a moron."

"What? I did—" he thought about it and the ugliness of it. He had said that to Evan.

His shoulders sunk. Looking at Stuart, he put his hand out. Stuart tossed the candy bar back.

"I'll apologize."

"He's not as strong as the rest of us, you know that."

"I know." Jason tore at the wrapper and took a bite, not tasting much.

"Jason," Stuart said.

Stuart never called him by his name. Jason stopped chewing and stared, watching Stuart search for the words.

"No one can put a time limit on grief."

"What are you talking about?"

"It's been fourteen months and we've been watching you. You seem stuck and can't push forward. How do we help you with that?"

"Leaving me the fuck alone."

"We're not set up for that."

"And you think you can help?"

"I don't know what you lost then or now, but I know how to grieve. My dad died when I was ten."

"You're the expert," Jason snapped. "You tell me how to make this stop, because I can't. I fucked up and I can't fix it."

"Jason, she's in a better place. You know that. She got old. Probably hurt. I mean more than just what you did to her."

"What?" Jason snapped again. He couldn't believe those words had come out of that mouth.

"Aye, you wanted her to hang around waiting for what? A brother who wasn't going to show up?"

Jason stared at him, feeling his anger accelerate. Wouldn't be the first time the Scotsman pissed him off to blows, but it had been awhile.

"I know how you feel," Stuart said. "We all do. It's not like this doesn't happen all the time."

Jason leaned a little closer, his eyes narrowing. "Not to me."

Stuart shrugged a shoulder and smiled. "So, plant a tree in her name. We're in the bloody forest. Should be room. If not, a rose bush in the backyard. We can dry one of the blooms when you have to leave her behind."

It didn't take more than that to have Jason tackling Stuart, sending them both back against the wall. He wanted the Scotsman to shut the fuck up. He should not be talking about Nancy. Not like this, not like anything.

The blows rained as they crashed around the room.

He got Stuart pinned to the ground and Jason landed three straight on punches to Stuart's face, screaming in wordless rage as he did it.

It was Travis who grabbed him, yanked him off Stuart. Jason didn't resist, he fell against Travis and watched Evan and Quinn move to Stuart. Blood smeared Stuart's face from his nose and mouth, marring his cheeks.

And thinking back, Jason didn't remember Stuart putting up all that much of a fight.

Evan picked up a broken potted plant, the plant falling out of the hole to land on the carpet. "Good job, Jason," Evan said.

And Stuart moved way too slow.

Jason closed his eyes. "Fuck," Jason said.

"Feel better?" Travis asked.

Sticky red blood covered Jason's hands. Droplets from the spray marred his sleeves.

"Fuck you," Jason snapped. He scrambled to his feet and moved away from all of them. Stuart was still on his back, his eyes closed. There was more blood on him than Jason.

"It wasn't a joke," Travis said. "You've been a powder keg for months. You needed to fix it but he didn't tell us he was going to do this."

Jason looked at Travis. "He did it on purpose?"

"Yeah, I think he did. We can ask him after we figure out if he has all his teeth."

Stuart knelt with Quinn's help and spit blood on the wood floor. "Wouldn't waste my time," Stuart said.

Quinn smiled. "Of course not."

"Jason," Travis said. "We've been watching and we took a vote. We like the old you better and we have to find a way to get you there."

"Why? Kick me out for this." He motioned to Stuart.

Stuart righted himself onto his knees. Quinn took a shoulder.

Evan grabbed one of the overturned chairs and brought it over for him.

Quinn stood straight. "Probably a couple of cracked ribs, at least."

"And that's what you want?" Travis asked Jason. "Lose us, too? You would be alone because a den won't take you unless you want to start murdering people again."

"You could go for me next," Quinn said, his gaze disappointed. "I think I can take you. Then you can move around the room and kick the shit out of everyone who cares about you."

"I want it over." Jason shouted.

"Then make it over."

The scarf on her head had more effect than the red manicured nails.

Jason didn't care. He wasn't here to date the chick. It was just about fifteen hours since he beat up one of his closest friends. The fact Stuart had set himself up as handy punching bag, made the guilt harder.

Jason laid down his hundred dollar bill, his fee to find what he needed.

Solace against the pain he couldn't shake.

Forgiveness from a woman—a sister—too far away to reach.

The woman squeezed his hand, a soft caress. "You've done this before?" she said. "Sought help. But without success."

The scent of incense hung on the enclosed patio. Plants and colored silk made up the majority of the area.

He held her hands and stared at the sapphire colored tablecloth.

"Couple times," he said.

"She says to stop."

Jason's gaze came up to stare at the pale woman with closed eyes.

"She says it's not helping you. And she says…wait…she looks just like you."

Shock had Jason returning the squeeze.

It was her—Isabella, the psychic—who broke contact and leaned back in her chair.

"You went to others for this same chance?"

Jason leaned back. "Not really. I never thought it would work."

"Then why did you try?"

He stared at the table a long time before lifting his gaze. "Because it hurts too much to know I won't have that chance I never took."

"She's close. You have to know that. You can tell without slapping down your cash or wishing her away. Because that's what you are doing, isn't it?"

He snapped to attention. "It doesn't matter what I am trying to do."

"She knows now," Isabella said. "Why you left, Jason."

He stared at her perplexed.

"I didn't tell you my name," he said.

"You didn't have to. She says she hurt for you all those years, not knowing. Now she knows and she knows you feel that pain. Pain you think you deserve."

Jason stared at the woman, weighing the words that made sense. He had been looking for them. He wanted to believe them.

"Who?" he said, feeling the apprehension.

"She knows you don't believe in me."

"Who?" Jason snapped.

"Your sister. Younger. She adored you. She still does."

"Did you talk to anyone?" Jason asked. "Anyone I know?"

"Let it go, she says, Live your life. But don't forget her."

Like that was possible.

It was also the last thing Nancy had said to him the day he boarded that bus for back east. A sense of serenity came into him, making his chest feel warm, his insides heal.

He didn't believe in bullshit, but sometimes, someone who was supernatural themselves, had to wonder if it was possible.

"She'll wait for you." Isabella said. "Even if it takes three hundred years."

Jason shoved away from the table and stood, staring down at the woman who stared back.

He reached in his back pocket, pulled out his wallet and opened it.

"You see her again," he said, "you tell her I never did and I never will."

He dropped four one hundreds next to the one already on the table. He pulled his leather jacket off the chair and put it on, thinking of the bakery on Foothill Avenue. It wasn't that far out of the way going home and if he knocked on the bakery door, the owner would open.

They had the best Scottish Shortbread in town.

Doctor's Orders

1996

Vampire hearing.

Could be a curse. Could be a blessing.

Standing outside the building on campus, Quinn waited for his ride. Since his truck was in the garage under Evan's watchful eye, Travis had agreed to pick Quinn up.

Rarely a day passed when Quinn didn't think about the reason he was in this place, doing what he was doing, because four other people thought it was a good idea. Not once in the last three and half years with this nursing program had any of them complained about having to live in snow county, having to shovel driveways in December or the fact Quinn hadn't earned a dime toward his 45% of the house budget since they had moved into the Arizona mountains to be near the school.

Standing in the fall cool mountains, Quinn heard the soft sniffles. He angled his head to listen better.

The last of all the students were gone by now, street lamps were lit. He looked to his left, tracking the sound of weeping.

Shouldn't be any of his business, but that didn't matter. He hiked his backpack up another inch and moved towards the direction of the sounds.

Michelle hid in the shadows. Quinn looked around, noting they were the last two waiting to go home. She stared at the ground, not seeing him. He moved close, slow as not to startle her.

"Michelle?" he said softly.

The jump didn't match the circumstances, putting him on alert.

"Michelle, what's wrong?"

"I thought everyone was gone."

"I was waiting for my ride. Are you okay?"

He stepped toward her. She stepped back.

He stopped in his place.

"Michelle, what's wrong?"

She looked at the ground, rolling her eyes. "I live about five blocks away but to get there I have to walk through Cinder Lane. I've always done it, since I've been in school."

Cinder Lane, the treed walking path running through campus. The very dark tree lined walking path with too many large bushes, shady areas and a reputation for trouble the campus liked to ignore.

He moved forward as her gaze darted to him. She flinched when he raised his hand to put on her shoulder.

"Michelle, you know you're safe, right?" he said. "I won't let anyone hurt you."

"He didn't hurt me," she said, soft.

"What did he do?" Quinn asked, feeling the heat burn low in his gut. Sexual offenses were not allowed in the society. The penalty was death.

She didn't answer.

"Did you call the police?"

Her gaze snapped to his. "He didn't do anything. He didn't touch me or hurt me. I don't know if it was wrong."

It was enough to get her terrified to walk home. And she missed two classes. Quinn was willing to bet whoever he was, he did it three nights ago.

"Why don't you tell me enough to keep you comfortable and I will tell you if that was bad?"

"He took my clothes."

"He took your clothes?" Quinn asked in rapid fire.

She nodded.

"Your scarf, jacket?"

He noticed for the first time she was in jeans. Michelle always wore skirts with thick tights, usually boots.

"He made me take off my boots and my stockings and then my panties."

She looked up at Quinn, her chin down, her eyes watery. "It was cold," she whispered. "He took my panties. And he played with them and made me watch."

Quinn closed his eyes, reminded himself she needed help first and he could rip the bastard apart later. Quinn took deep breaths.

"He had a gun."

Held her at gunpoint. Forced her out of her unmentionables. Played with—Quinn cut his thought off and went with yes. He had hurt her. Bad and the tears on her face were proof enough.

"What are you doing over here?" Travis asked as he walked up. "I've been waiting ten minutes in the parking lot."

Quinn motioned behind with a hand to stop. Travis did.

"Michelle?"

She stared over Quinn's shoulder.

"Michelle, this is Travis. I live with Travis. He's a great guy and he won't hurt you either, okay?"

Quinn reached up to run a hand on her short hair.

"Travis," he said, without taking his gaze off Michelle. "Call the police."

Half hour later Quinn stood at the back of the classroom beside Travis, while an officer quizzed Michelle on the events two nights ago.

"You were walking home?" the officer asked.

Michelle, seated at one of the tables where they usually took notes in class, nodded.

"It was after class," the cop said. "Very dark. Late and you walked home alone?"

Her gaze came up and Quinn didn't blame her. The tone of that question sorta pissed him off.

"Do you have a plan with that line of questioning?" Quinn asked.

"You're here out of courtesy. Don't irritate me."

Quinn, his arms folded on his chest, looked up at Travis. Travis stared back.

"He's saying I'm irritating him," Quinn said to Travis.

"You've been known to do that."

Quinn stared, then looked at the door and turned back to Travis. Travis followed his gaze, then moved toward the closed door, blocking Cop 2 from entering if he came back too soon.

"You said you had on a skirt," the cop asked.

"I always wear skirts."

"How short was it?"

"Hey," Quinn snapped off the wall. "You don't want to take that line of questioning. Face me."

As predicted, the cop turned in his seat to glare directly at Quinn. And even the distance couldn't stop Quinn from capturing the cop's full attention before he could bark an order.

"It's not the first time, is it?" Quinn asked, moving closer, while Michelle leaned back in her chair.

"There's been rumors," the cop said.

"How many rumors?"

"Six before this. Over the last six months."

Quinn bit off a swear and looked at the floor. "Why wasn't the school informed?"

"It's a tourist town," the cop said. "And a lot of college kids. We don't want the bad press. Besides, it's not like anyone got hurt."

Quinn's head snapped up and he took a step forward.

"Quinn," Travis said. "No. It's not him."

"But he's handy. And no one will get hurt."

"I happen to know you and know someone will get hurt."

They had been in the mountains for almost four years, enjoying the benefits—and non-benefits—of four seasons.

They had to throw down with paper, scissors, rock to figure out who would shovel the driveway around five cars in various shapes

Quinn stood at the coffee pot, his mind not on his finals.

He had been in love once. The kind of love that a person—or vampire—didn't find twice. Anna should have been his wife. Six weeks before the wedding she became his memory.

Sexual misconduct was a big time vampire no-no. Quinn took a drink of his black brew and thought of Anna's little sister, Becky. She had been caught one day on the path home by two teenage boys. What the boys actually did was not mentioned in polite society, but enough was known for Quinn to carry his right to judgment into this life.

Just one more semester of night classes and he would again have a medical degree and be able to work in hospitals in a way that didn't require a mop.

Every day he appreciated what his family did. Whether it was going to their various jobs for income or pulling extra duties at home.

Jason sat at the dining room table, reading from the papers in front of him.

"Why do you think your patient has pneumonia?" Jason asked.

Quinn had a review today. Like hell anyone would let him forget it.

"Fever. Trouble breathing. They're not looking all that great so I thought I would take a minute to get a chest x-ray."

Jason's gaze shifted to Quinn's. "That's how you word it? A little sarcasm to go with their penicillin?"

"I don't prescribe but if I did, I would stay away from that one." His smile matched his derision.

"What would you use?" Stuart asked from across the table.

"A sharp object," Quinn smiled again.

"What are you doing?" Jason asked.

Quinn sat forward on the chair. "What the fuck are you doing? I know the test. I don't want to be drilled on the test. I want to know what we are going to do about it."

"Technically it's not our problem. The police have to do this."

"We slip up and we might get noticed," Stuart added.

Quinn looked between them, shifting from one gaze to the other.

There was no way in hell either of these two would let a woman get hurt if it was within their reach to stop it.

"What have you been doing?" he asked Jason.

"Helping you study." Jason said into his coffee.

He looked at Stuart. No expression.

Quinn looked around the room, then checked his watch. He looked at Jason.

"Where's Travis?"

"Worked late. He called when you were in the shower."

"And Evan?"

"Probably the same," Jason said. He picked up the exam.

"Medical treatment of coronary artery disease includes…" He looked at Quinn.

"You guys have been patrolling the lane."

The silent pause lasted too long.

"Yeah," Jason finally laughed. "Not exactly walk away material."

"Why didn't you tell me?" Quinn snapped.

Jason held up the study sheets. "It's actually the reason we're living at this altitude."

The phone rang, was answered and handed off to Quinn.

Quinn took the call, and put the phone back down, the fury racing across his nerves. Jill was just this side of the sweetest thing ever. To put a hand on her in anger or worse, Quinn's own hand shook.

"What's going on?"

"Jill was jumped last night in the commons, heading back to her apartment."

Quinn looked up at Jason.

"What?" Jason asked.

Quinn looked at the clock.

Jason held up the papers, facing them toward Quinn.

"Medical treatment of coronary artery disease includes…" Jason smiled.

Quinn hit the lane after the test. Calls to check-in at home told him that everyone under his roof was out tonight. Every section of Cinder Lane would be controlled.

One way or another, this bastard would be stopped.

It wasn't vampire skills that narrowed his search. It was knowing where the hunting ground lay, between the light posts twenty and thirty-seven. The trees were thicker, the shadows longer.

When he heard the sound of another girl weep, Quinn had his mark. He came from the left, catching a guy with a girl pinned by a tree. Quinn slammed the redheaded bastard against the trunk. The kid, maybe twenty, shook under Quinn's hand, held at the neck.

The girl fell to the ground.

"Catlin is a friend of mine. A close friend," Quinn said. "And I don't think I like what you were doing to her."

"Wasn't anything," the kid stuttered. "It's a friggin' game."

Quinn reached in his pocket, had the knife out, and brought it to the kid's throat. Quinn would worry about Catlin's memories later.

"Quinn, don't." Travis's voice snapped behind him.

"Sexual misconduct," Quinn said. "That's a death sentence and you know it."

He did not take his gaze off this son-of-a-bitch, the fury hotter than it had been in a long time. He wanted this kid to pay with blood.

He felt the change inside that happened when he 'showed'.

"Oh my God, what are you?" The voice hit high pitched, the shaking hitting hard.

The kid pulled at Quinn's arm, trying to break free.

Travis came close. "We can't choose which laws we obey and which we toss."

"Sure we can," Quinn said. "We do it all the time."

"Not on murder."

Quinn swung his face to Travis. "Murder? He's a sexual predator who will do this again as soon as he gets out. This is justice."

"We don't do it like before," Travis said. "You make him think he's a raccoon who dry humps trees, I don't care. But we give us up if we take the kill."

His fingers squeezing the neck in his hands, Quinn took deep breaths, trying to bring it in. Quinn's chin lowered, his eyes closed. It was a scenario in his mind he had lived through the decades. Safety for her, a pardon for him.

And they weren't those people anymore. Not being those people was why four friends worked their asses off so he could have his wish.

With a heavy, audible breath, he dropped his hand and took a step back.

He spoke to the kid while Travis knelt beside a crying and shivering Catlin.

"You're going to stand against that tree until the police arrive. No rent-a-cop. The police and then you are going to confess."

"I'll tell them everything."

Quinn's shoulders sagged. The knowledge he had got the kid to stop slammed into the knowledge he would always regret he didn't take the kill.

"Last box in kitchen," Evan yelled from somewhere in the house.

"Put it in the garage. I think we can start loading the van in the morning."

His mattress and box spring leaned against the wall, the frame dismantled.

The medical supplies he had acquired were packed in a box, a big red X on the outside.

Being a doctor was all he had ever wanted to be. When he was a kid, when he was in school, after the vampires turned him and murdered Anna.

There had been no more attacks on Cinder Lane. The guilty Gilbert Henry sat in jail.

Quinn glanced out the window, smelling the pine.

The weekend of moving, a long planned event, always brought about a feeling of nostalgia. In a few days he would be staring at a new ceiling.

Quinn picked up the envelope that came in the mail. The diploma was still sealed inside. He didn't have to look.

"My room's done," Jason said from the door. "What do you need?"

Quinn's head snapped up, looking at Jason. "What?"

Jason stepped into the room, eyeing Quinn. "What's up?"

Quinn ran his tongue over his teeth, and held up the envelope.

"First graduation in Boston, I thought I was hell on wheels. I was going to change the world with Anna."

"Bad word," Jason said. "You know that's a bad word. We don't say that word."

"You want to know the truth?" Quinn asked.

Jason shrugged.

Quinn paused. He looked Jason in the eye. "I lost more with that degree, but I think I got something more here."

"Do you know you're not making sense?"

"I think this spring with what he did to those girls, it dredged up things I didn't want to remember."

"We can burn your certificate and stop payment on the check for the state."

Quinn smiled, turned the manila envelope over in his hand.

He looked around the room and then over to Jason. "It's all packed up. I just need to grab a few important things."

He moved to the nightstand, opened the drawer for the Bible. When he had stolen it from Anna's mom after the funeral, his conscious had already shifted to vampire. Back then he didn't care if it had hurt her as long as he got the book.

"You can think all you want but you know the pieces will never come together, right?" Jason asked.

Quinn looked over his shoulder at Jason, still here.

Quinn looked at the book, again. He slid his finger between the cover and the first page.

The one photo he still had was glued to the inside. Anna's smiling face stared at him in black and white.

He held up the Bible. "Deliverance. That's what they call it when a vampire turns us into them. Our Deliverance Day."

Jason leaned his shoulder onto the jamb.

"She had a sister," Quinn said quietly. He looked at Jason. "I never told you that."

"No, you never did."

He stared at the book. "We put off the wedding by a year because Rebecca had…" He looked at Jason. "They didn't rape her but there was enough damage that it mattered. Anna was beside herself, wanted to fix it."

"You would have died married."

"Yeah, I guess."

Jason stepped into the room. "This is what keeps you on edge when it's Law #5."

"She was thirteen, Jason."

"I don't care if she was forty-five. No woman deserves that. I'm just understanding you a little better."

Quinn smiled and chuckled. "Good luck."

"You know, when we get settled in the new place, I can probably find some records on Anna's sister, see what happened to her."

Quinn stared at the book, flipped it closed and thought of what he could gain from knowing.

"No," he said. "It's history."

"It's fucked up and undeserved. You should stop worrying about it."

Quinn slapped his hand on the back of the book. "Grab the boxes."

Quinn went to the duffle bag on a box and shoved the Bible on top of his folded jeans.

Collateral Damage

1999

Alice was a new addition to his routine, one seen on a semi regular basis for the last two months.

Stuart stayed the night with her three weeks to the day of meeting her.

Not his usual style.

He liked to go slow. He liked to not rush.

But he had come out after a shift, found her sitting on his bike following weeks of serving her rums and Cokes. Not ready to jump into anything, he was interested enough to take that first kiss she offered.

She wanted more. Fast.

She was sweet, he thought. The kind of girl he might consider for fun times with. Brown hair, brown eyes with a smooth complexion. He liked the feel of her, the taste. She fit perfectly in ways that mattered.

Leaving her to sleep for a few more minutes before he had to go home, he dressed quietly, touching her long hair before grabbing his shoes to put on in the living room.

He sat down on the couch, picked up the first black athletic shoe and began to pull it on.

He was tying the second when the pile of magazines caught his eye on the coffee table. Under them, he saw only the edge of a manila folder and enough of *'Stuar…'* in the heading to catch his attention.

He reached over, pushed the magazines aside and found an entire file with his name in bold print across the top. He stared at it, piecing reluctant parts together. On the table were pens and a yellow pad. She had been working here when he had come over unannounced last night, asking for a date.

She turned him down to going out, but didn't have a problem with them staying in.

Flipping through the pages he felt the nausea rise up to choke his throat.

Okay with mirrors.

Loves the pasta I made with tons of garlic.

Had to pause at front door until I asked him in.

Holy fuck, he thought, turning the pages faster, catching the words in a blur.

Jason Sullivan involved with Rebecca Sanchez. Have notified her of what he is.

Evan, not sure. Still debating. Has to be one to be there in that crowd.

Travis didn't turn me down when I asked him to buy me a drink. Nice eyes, but avoid teeth.

Because you are not his type, Stuart thought to himself.

The back pages listed vampire hunting sites around the country with contact numbers. Notes marred the margins in purple and green ink.

She picked him up, he thought, flipping back to start over. All their names were listed. She came into the bar, then waited for him. She asked him to dinner, to her place.

And he had said yes.

Holding the files, he turned on the couch. She was ten feet behind him, watching.

He saw the lie in everything she said.

"Work go okay at the flower shop today?" he asked.

She looked at the folder in his hand.

"I knew I should have told you," she said.

"Tell me that you don't work with flowers?"

"I'm a reporter. For the Spokane Herald."

His voice froze for a second as bad went to worse. "A reporter?"

"Well, I'm going to be. Right now I work in the advertising division but they told me if I bring in a good story, they'll let me write it. "

He laughed. "And you think this is a good story? You think anyone will believe this shit? Your facts don't even add up."

"They don't have to. Not perfect, anyway. The people I spoke to told me some things are myth and might be off from what we see in fiction."

"And who told you this?"

"Mostly? I talked to a guy with this British group. Cost me a fortune in phone bills. Night Shadows, they're called. He knew a lot about you."

"About me? You think you found vampires living in Spokane? You're nuts."

"Don't even try, Stuart. I already know everything I need to."

He focused on how to fix it and not explain it. "What the fuck does that mean?"

"The guy who talked to me said that vampires like to use blood sport in sex. Why didn't you ever do that with me?"

"What?" Stuart gasped.

"I might have liked that. I've never done that."

"Maybe because you're crazy and I'm leaving?"

"I met Travis. Jason, too. They both have bars they like. Wasn't too hard to get them to buy me a drink."

Stuart took a step toward her. "Stay away from my family."

"Family? Really?" she laughed. "You're related to them? Because you always told me they were just roommates."

"We're not people you want to test for patience."

"My editor is going to love this," she smiled. "I have waited so long for a break. Then you walk in." She smiled more. "I have an appointment with him to present all this the day after tomorrow. I had to almost kill for that appointment."

"And you figured all this out how?"

"I had to piece it together," she said. "I followed you home even before we met."

"You liked *Buffy*? *Lost Boys*? This is where you're getting your information?"

"No. There's a couple of underground groups in the country, a couple in England. They were happy to help when I told them what I had."

"What you had?" he asked, soft. "What you had was a lover in your bed who liked the feel of you."

"So? I don't care. Don't you get it? This story could make something of me. It's what I've always wanted."

"Do you understand? Publishing it could destroy what chance we have?"

She shrugged one shoulder. "Collateral damage," she said. "I don't care about you. I don't care about your friends. I want this chance."

"Did you tell them about us? These groups?"

"I told them I had you. I told them what city I was in. I didn't tell them any names."

"Because giving them our names might give them the story."

She smiled.

There was a time in his life when he was a good judge of character, especially with woman.

"You fucked your way into a story," Stuart said.

"It's not like it was all bad. You seemed to know what you were doing."

She stared at his nose, over his shoulder, above his head. None of those positions made him feel better.

"Look at me," he said. He had one way to walk away clean with no worries.

"No," she said. "The guy in England told me about that. You can make me think things and do things just by looking at me. You're not taking this from me."

His one chance vanished. Killing her was next on the list of solutions—only he couldn't kill her. He didn't have that choice anymore. He couldn't turn her and live with his conscience, not with what they had all accomplished at the house. He had to bet on Jason and that computer.

They had to run.

All five of them.

Tonight.

Stuart walked to the dining room table, grabbing his coat to pull it on.

"What did you think, Stuart? Till death do us part? We were having fun. Now I can make more fun."

He turned to look at her, thought of about ten responses, then figured she wasn't worth any of them.

He left without a word, his hands fisted in the pockets of his jacket, his mind racing, calculating how fast they could get out of here.

He was up to the intersection when he heard her call him. He kept walking, into the street, across to the other side.

"Stuart," she cried. "I have to do this. You know I have to."

He didn't know why she followed. He didn't know why she felt she had to tell him.

He just knew he was almost to the other side of the street when he turned to stare at her coming toward him, already on the asphalt.

When the car sped around Laguna Street onto Greenwich she was in the intersection.

With that mere second to think yes or no, life or death, he made the decision. Her or them...because if she lived, they would go down.

Jason wouldn't be able to plan escape fast enough.

Stuart had the chance. He could have done it.

He didn't.

With his eyes shut tight and his whole body tense and suddenly covered with a fine layer of sweat, he listened to the brakes, her scream and the thud as metal slammed into flesh.

Breathing heavy, Stuart opened his eyes. The car stopped after a skid of black in the road, the driver got out yelling at Alice to get up, his stagger and misstep proof of the alcohol that caused this.

Alice was thrown some distance on the road, her body twisted, one arm down, one out from her side.

He didn't have to check. The blood by her head was already a confirmation to whatever internal injuries she suffered.

"Why won't she get up?" The drunk screamed. A few people came out in the early hours from the apartments.

Someone said they had called for an ambulance.

Stuart dropped to one knee beside her. He ran a hand over her hair, thinking how good it had been to be with her, while she had probably been faking most of it.

"Were you a witness?" someone asked.

"Aye," he said, soft. "I saw the whole thing."

"What's your name?"

"Peterson, Russ Peterson," Stuart said. He looked up at the guy and watched him write that down.

"Did you know her?"

He paused even though he already knew his answer. "No," Stuart said. "I was just walking by."

Stuart came in the backdoor.

Travis waited. "What the fuck do you think you're doing?" He looked at his watch. "It's two minutes until sunrise."

"Is it?" Stuart asked, breathless. He looked around the room.

Jason sat at the table with his new Toshiba Satellite laptop, staring at Stuart instead of playing with the buttons. In the other room, Stuart could hear Quinn and Evan laugh with the television.

"What's wrong?" Travis asked.

Stuart shot his gaze up. "What?"

"What?" Travis said again.

Stuart thought, debated as he had the whole walk home. That was six miles ago.

"The girl I was seeing," he finally said.

"Alice Something."

"Reynolds," he said. "I was there tonight."

"Any good?" Jason jabbed.

Stuart looked at Travis without answering Jason. "She said she met you. You had a drink with her."

Travis shrugged. "Did I? I don't remember any Alice. And I'm pretty sure you know I wouldn't be hitting on your girlfriend."

Stuart tilted his chin. "No, it wasn't about you. She knew about us. She had files. She's been watching all of us for a while. She told me she worked in a flower shop, but it was a lie. She was a reporter." He laughed hard. "She picked me up because she knew what I was and wanted to find out more. She was going to expose us."

Jason shut the laptop as Quinn and Evan came in.

"Um, Stuart," Jason said. "Are you even aware you are talking about her in the past tense?" He looked up at him.

"She knew about us," Stuart said again. "She was going to expose us for a story. She was fucking sleeping with me to get closer. She hit on most of you and you don't even remember because it was too unimportant. But me? She zeroed in and I fell for it."

"She's dead?" Quinn asked.

Stuart waited and then nodded. "About two hours ago."

"What happened?" Travis asked.

"I left the apartment when I found out. She followed. I was almost across the street when she stepped into the intersection. The car came out of nowhere. The guy was drunk. She was dead when I got to her."

He went to the fridge, pulled out a beer and drank it to half.

"I could have saved her," he said soft, lowering the beer bottle.

"You had the time?" Travis asked.

"Aye," Stuart said, looking at Travis. "I walked out and left her alive when I could have done it there. I couldn't even suggest. She knew about it and wouldn't look me in the eye. And four minutes later, I watched her die."

"You didn't kill her," Quinn said.

"Didn't I? If you don't stop it, aren't you just as guilty of starting it?"

"You described an accident," Jason said. "You didn't do that."

"She knew I wouldn't kill her. I couldn't do it. I could have turned her."

"No, you couldn't. You're not that thing anymore," Evan said.

"I could have stopped it. I could have gotten to her."

"You're sure she's dead?"

He nodded. "The blood spread in feet, not inches."

"I am sorry, this is going to hurt for a long time," Travis said. "But if what you said is true, didn't you trade a liar for the five of us?"

"Does that make it right?"

"No. And it never will. We walk away."

Stuart looked at Jason. "How long to put it together?"

"We've only been here four years."

"She talked to vampire hunters," Stuart said. "Can you hide us?"

Jason bobbed his head with a nod. "I don't see a problem."

"She had a computer like yours. I went back to her place to make sure I didn't leave anything. I poured water into it then grabbed all the papers. I threw them in the sewer on my way back here."

"That will work," Jason said. "And good thinking."

"They have nothing to trace us with," Travis said.

"I can divert some information to hide us," Jason said.

"It's because of me," Stuart said. "All of you have to pick up and run because of me."

"And in 1965," Quinn said, "it was because of me. We adapt."

"Can I get a puppy at the new house?" Evan asked because he always asked.

"No," four voices sounded as one.

"We're good?" Travis asked. "Jason, do it."

Cross Over

2002

Two hours into his nightly game, Evan saw the same man in the same suit come onto the playground. He waved but Evan ignored him.

"Shit," Evan muttered under his breath. He shot his twenty-five footer for game.

It was a pick-up game in a park about twenty minutes from the house. Pick-up games were easy to get into. If he wasn't going to be at this park, there was another or a rec center offering the same sport. There was comradery between kids who just wanted to play. Every player here, whether winning or losing tonight, patted each other on the back as they cleared the court to make way for the next game.

Good game.

When can we play again?

Evan slid his glance to the man on the bleachers. Three days, three visits. The message never. Evan's response was never heard.

The family he lost, they echoed in his mind daily. The family he had now, he had adapted and he trusted they knew what was best for him in a life he didn't always understand.

The man left the bleachers and walked toward him. "Man—Harris. What a shot! Did you see that shot?" His face beamed with a bright smile. A smile with an edge of 'we can do this.' His hands moved as he spoke, trying to keep up with his fast pace.

Evan ignored him, moving to the benches lining the court where his duffle bag lay. He put his ball down, and grabbed the bag, yanking down the zipper to pull out his sweats.

"You have got to be interested in pursuing this as a career."

"Not really," Evan said, as he had said the last two nights to the same offers.

"You're a natural. You can't waste this." He laughed and used his hands some more. "You could make this a career after college."

Evan zipped up his hoodie and turned to face the man.

"Mr. Roberts, I already told you. I appreciate your offer but I'm not going to college."

"Four years with nothing to worry about but grades, girls and ball? You're not going to get anything better."

Evan knew the deal. It had been offered before by a man very much Roberts. Eager, wanting to further his own career by recruiting the best. Evan was the best, Roberts said.

"Your game is good. Lots of hops. You can dunk and for someone your height…"

Evan looked at him. "I'm tall enough. If I do that good than I'm tall enough. And I'm still not going to college. You'll have to leave me alone."

"Can I talk to your parents?"

"My parents won't try to talk me into anything I've already said no to. Now, will you leave me alone?"

The scout's expression shifted. "Fucking waste. You got all this talent and you won't use it. You're wasting it on what? Grand Theft Auto?"

Evan reached over and picked up his duffle. "If you are still around here, I will find another place to play. I don't need your selfish one-eyed shit. I don't want to play for you. You understand?"

"No, I don't understand," he snapped. "You're throwing away something you want and that's just fucking stupid."

Evan turned and headed across the asphalt.

"Harris…" Roberts yelled. Evan didn't turn.

Because Evan knew he was lying. He had spent years honing his skills to do exactly what this guy was offering. A 'yes' sounded real good if he could figure out a way to go to college in daylight hours.

He sighed hard as he hit the sidewalk and started for home.

"What was that about?"

Evan stopped and turned. Stuart sat on the wall of someone's rose garden. You could just smell the blooms.

"What are you doing here?"

"Trying to figure what put the weight of the world on your shoulders."

"What?"

"You've been acting off the last few days. I decided to find the source. I didn't catch everything he said, but could tell it bothered you."

"It's not bothered. It's pissed."

Stuart hopped down to stand next to Evan.

"What made you this pissed?"

Evan looked at him, wondering if he really had to answer.

"I wanted to say yes," Evan said. "It was this whole life I imagined when I was in school. Class, practice, dating. I didn't get it."

"I'm sorry, Evan," Stuart said. "That wasn't fair."

Evan stared at him, knowing Stuart held a portion of responsibility for where Evan stood now. If not for him and Travis, Evan would have died.

"He offered me a full ride, four years to State. No money worries."

Stuart smiled. "Is there anything that will make this easier on you?"

Evan turned to face Stuart.

"I stopped counting years ago," Evan said.

"Counting what?"

Evan shrugged. "How many days it had been. When one of their birthday's came by. Christmas, everything. Stuart, I know what happened was fucked. That night, if I had taken a different route to the parking lot, I wouldn't have been in the wrong place at a wrong time."

Stuart stared but didn't answer.

Evan continued. "And if you hadn't been in that bar that night, or Travis hadn't opened the door—all of us would have ended up in a different place."

"You're sounding very reasonable."

Evan glanced down and smiled. He looked up. "I hate that it happened and I bet you still do, too."

Stuart shrugged.

"I can't change it," Evan said. He pointed over his shoulder to the scout. "I can't be what he wants. I know that. I need to be here, doing what I'm doing with the family I have."

Stuart pursed his lips a little, and nodded slowly. He reached into his jacket pocket and pulled out a plastic storage box and a fork.

"What's that?"

"I thought I might have to cheer you up but you sound fine," he told Evan.

"What's that?"

"The last piece of chocolate cake Travis brought home from the bakery."

Laughing, Evan grabbed and pulled open the lid.

Brother from Another Mother

1985

The car hotwired, Stuart took the city streets faster than this damp road should allow.

Next to him, in the passenger's seat, Travis leaned back, his eyes closed, his breathing too shallow. Blood soaked his shirt and covered his leather coat.

The smell of it emanated off his clothes.

Stuart didn't want red lights. He wanted this nightmare over. Karma couldn't have this big of a hotspot against their kind for them to fail.

Stuart's breath caught in his chest aching as he faced the reality of this whole lot of blood. It was coming from a slice in Travis' neck and vampire and neck slice wasn't a good combination.

But that was a shitload of blood staining the leather seats in Travis' Firebird.

Travis hadn't spoken a word since they got into the car. The first aid Stuart gave at his date's house wasn't enough.

Keeping the speed slower now, he came down the alley and turned into Travis' spot outside the house. Stuart was out

127

of the car and around to Travis' side. Pulling the door open, Stuart unbuckled the seat belt and Travis' big frame jerked as he leaned out the door.

With Travis unconscious, there were limited ways to move him while not worsening the wound.

Stuart ran to the back door of the house, stepped into the kitchen and found Jason playing cards with Evan.

"Now," Stuart snapped.

They turned to look at him. "What?"

"I need help." He ran back to the car, Jason and Evan behind him.

"Shit, is he dead?"

"No," Jason said. "No ashes."

"Help me get him inside."

Jason snapped at Evan. "Call the hospital. Have them page Quinn with an emergency. Tell them to tell him *Fuzzy Slippers.*"

Fuzzy Slippers. Password to be home now.

"I know, I know," Evan said, running up the stairs.

Jason took one side, Stuart the other. Travis' feet dragged behind them.

"He smells like smoke."

Stuart didn't answer.

"You went to the bar to pick up chicks," Jason said. "Travis said it was a sure thing."

"It wasn't a sure thing," Stuart said.

They got him on the couch and Stuart checked the measly bandage he had tied. It was soaked through. He left it in place and went to get a small towel.

"What happened?" Jason snapped.

"We went back to the house with these girls. It seemed—"

"—it seemed what?"

"I went upstairs then came down to get him. Chick's boyfriend was behind me. He said some whacked shit. His knife was bloody and the downstairs was on fire."

Jason chuckled. "You know, I've planned dates like that but they never turn out."

Stuart glared at him.

"The boyfriend?"

"Thought a frontal assault would be better with me. Near as I can figure out, Travis was making out and that guy came in from behind."

"The boyfriend?"

"Guy was unconscious in the hallway when I dragged Travis out. Building was engulfed by the time I got the car hotwired."

Jason narrowed his eyes.

"Wallet, keys. They were gone," Stuart said. "I didn't have time to search."

"Anyone else in the house?"

"I don't know. I grabbed him and—there wasn't time, Jason. There wasn't time to check. I barely got us out."

Jason's gaze dropped to Stuart's torn shirt.

The phone rang in the kitchen. "That's Quinn calling back," Jason said.

"We're going to need blood. A shitload," Stuart said.

Family meant connections. It meant security and safety. Stuart had left the best he ever had in Scotland before he came to America. The family he had now, he would lay money that they would always have his back.

Travis lay on that bed, Quinn doing what Quinn did. Stuart returned to the Catholic prayers, of his youth knowing for certain they would never help.

Jason came out to the back porch, handing off a beer before taking the wooden chair next to Stuart.

"Fuckin' cold tonight," Jason said, resting his feet on the railing. "Quinn's finishing up and can give you the details. I think we might have gotten lucky."

Stuart drank from the beer, not tasting it. "I was leaning against the wall for a taxi when Travis came out. He was falling down drunk, laughing at his own stupidly. I took one glance and figured he looked good for dinner."

"You're talking about San Francisco?"

Stuart nodded and took another drink. "We've been together almost fifty years."

Jason smiled. "You followed him home?"

Stuart nodded. He smiled and looked at Jason. "I think the walk took longer than usual for him. He told me later, he'd stopped counting at nine beers."

"Big guy," Jason chuckled.

"A potentially good dinner," Stuart smiled. He looked at Jason. "None of us were supposed to figure it out."

"Figure what out?"

Stuart looked back into the dark. They were far enough off the road not to raise suspicion.

"Vampires are all about self-serv. We're not supposed to care enough about anything, including ourselves, to step in front of the train for someone else." He looked at Jason again. "You would do it for Quinn. You would do it for anyone of us. Hell, you would probably do it for me and you can't stand me half the time."

"No," Jason said, drinking. "It's all the time." He looked at Stuart. "I just like to throw you off."

Stuart smiled and drained his bottle.

Evan leaned out the door. "Quinn's done. He says to meet him in the kitchen."

Quinn had washed up and had a new shirt on by the time he joined the crowd.

"What the fuck did you do tonight?" Quinn asked Stuart, sharp.

Stuart looked up. "Picked up a couple of girls and went back to their house."

"I'm curious what a monk does with a one-night stand," Jason managed to grin.

Stuart tilted his chin but didn't answer Jason.

He spoke to Quinn.

"I don't know exactly what happened. Susan, that's the girl I was with, had an attic bedroom. I could already smell smoke but I honestly thought it was outside. I got to the door, this guy stops me. He was high or something. He had a bloody knife and when he started talking, I knew we were fucked."

The three of them watched him.

"I don't know who was in the house. I know this guy was out on the hall carpet because I put him there. I had to break in the door to get to Travis and by then, the smoke was coming up the stairs. You couldn't see two feet."

"This guy had purpose and knew how to cut," Quinn said, "but we're a little nastier. Travis is going to be stationary for a while."

"What do you mean?"

"He used all the blood I grabbed at the hospital," Quinn said. "I'm going out to get some more."

"I saw the news," Evan said. "There was a fire across town on Church Street. Were you on Church Street?"

"Aye," Stuart sighed.

"They found a body."

"Just one?" Stuart snapped.

Evan nodded.

"What do we do now?"

Quinn finished wiping his hands on the dark towel. "We wait and see how good I am."

Vampire accelerated healing worked in their favor. Stuart spent his nights in the chair in Travis' room examining the concept of a sworn enemy turned friend. The concept hadn't existed when he walked into the pub in New Orleans that night.

"You decided the night before," Stuart said. "When we were alone."

Still weak, Travis reached for the pad of paper on the nightstand and the sharpie. He wrote slowly. His near miss had been closer than any of them had ever had. It would be another few weeks before Travis spoke normally.

He turned the pad around for Stuart to read.

"What the fuck are you whining about?"

Stuart smiled and looked at the beer in his hands. The question wasn't exactly a surprise.

"The Dragon's Bridge," Stuart said, raising his gaze to Travis'.

Travis managed to growl. He slammed down the pad.

"What are you talking about?" he asked, his voice sounding like sand paper.

"How long did you think about what I suggested before deciding to come with me?"

Travis put his head on the pillow, his eyes narrowed, his response slow. "What?"

"The Dagon's Bridge?" Stuart asked again.

Travis shifted his gaze to the ceiling.

"Wanda," he managed, looking back at Stuart. "Did she get out?"

"No one but her boyfriend was left. I haven't tried to contact them."

"Better that way," Travis sighed, fading into the pillow. "Before the end of the first bottle," he said, watching Stuart.

"I think we've been sitting across the same breakfast table for a lot of decades. You get attached."

Travis smiled. "Is that what we are?"

Stuart drank and tried not to smile. "We're something, that's for sure." He looked down to the beer he held. He brought his gaze back up to Travis.

Travis still too pale, his eyes almost bloodshot.

"You know what, you pull a stunt like this again and I might finish the job." He smiled as he said it.

Travis grinned a little. "Yeah," he said. "You're handy to keep around, too."

Stuart stood up. "I have to go to work."

"Glad we had this talk." Travis grinned a little.

"I would tell you to fuck off, but it would take too much effort." He turned toward the door.

"Stuart?" Travis whispered.

Stuart stopped and looked at him.

"Thank you," Travis said.

"Fuck off," Stuart laughed, then turned to head out.

Meet Max
2009

It was the look in the eyes, Stuart thought from behind the bar. Something that rang untrue with a man he had never seen. In another life, this guy may have been good looking with his dark eyes. Right now, Stuart didn't see the looks. He saw the charm even from this distance. There was a way the other man moved, something calculated.

Bob Segar sang on the jute box, asking Stuart to put *Turn the Page* on speakers and it was loud enough not to hear what this guy was saying to the girl at the high table where she sat.

He was good. She was buying every line. She would walk out of the door with him to forbidden places and she would never know what happened.

Her name was Jenny. Coming into the bar with girlfriends was a weekly occurrence. At 5'2", she was sweet and a little bit gullible. It seriously would not take much to get her in the mood for some fun.

As Stuart set the beer in front of Every-Night-Craig, Stuart saw Jenny get up and move toward the door, her stranger on her elbow.

Stuart rang up Craig's bill and palmed the lime knife out of its holder.

"I'll be right back," he told Mike, the owner and fellow bartender.

Stuart passed by the people oblivious to what was outside. Anyone of them, male or female, could have been the one the stranger picked. Stuart stood outside the closed entrance door, thinking back to the days of his own hunting. Dark was preferable. Privacy, a necessity.

He walked around the building, passed Mike's Silverado, his own bicycle, then he heard voices and the gasp. He doubled his movements.

There is a brief instant in taking a victim when the hot blood coats the vampire's tongue. The taste, the texture, the heat…all envelop the vampire, creating a window of vulnerability as the food hits their system. Lasting only seconds, but it is then you can strike to take them down.

Stuart watched enough to make sure he had the advantage.

The knife in hand, he got close without being heard, then pushed only the tip into the guy's neck, the point digging in.

"You want to let her go?"

Hands dropped off Jenny. She staggered back.

"Don't," the man said in a panicked voice.

Stuart wanted to check Jenny, see how bad she was hurt. She sank against the wall, Stuart's free hand came up to hold the back of the neck of the vampire.

"I wasn't going to hurt her."

"A little foreplay out here? I can see her and damn well know what the hell you were after."

He grabbed the vampire by the throat and slammed him against the wall hard enough to rattle fangs. Keeping an eye on the near-coma Jenny, Stuart put the blade flush now against the vampire's neck.

"What," he sputtered, the blood still on his lips and coating his teeth. The fangs were retracted but it didn't hide what he was. "What? I liked her. She liked me."

"Yeah, I know," Stuart sneered.

"My wallet. It's in my back pocket. Take it. It's not much in there but the cards are good."

Stuart flared, showing what they always hid. It was there, and then it was gone.

"Fuck," the guy moaned. "No." The vampire's head fell back against the wall, his pale skin dropping a shade. "What now?"

"Where's your den?" Stuart asked, knife in place.

"I don't have one."

"You don't have a den? You're in town by yourself? Why would I believe you?"

"I haven't been in a den in years. Too many complications."

"What's your name?"

"Garcia," he said. "Maximilian Garcia."

"Max," Stuart said.

Max nodded. "I am not worth any of this. I don't kill 'em. I just get enough."

"When was the last time?"

"It's been weeks. I don't know how many. I was in Portland. Are you going to let me go?"

With the knife held in place, Stuart reached his other hand into his back pocket, taking out his phone. Still staring into the eyes of Max, he autodialed and waited.

"Thought you were at work," Travis said when he picked up.

"I need you to get your car and meet me behind Coopers."

"I'm at work."

"I need you to bring rope, duct tape and couple of stakes."

"Hey, I know you're a party animal, but tonight's not a good night for me."

"How long?"

"Half hour to pick up the shit, ten minute drive. I assume it's not a whim? You have a reason."

"Yeah," he drew out in his Scottish burr "His name is Max and he tried to eat a customer. I want to take him home and see what he is willing to tell."

"I will tell you anything," Max whined.

"Shut up," Stuart said.

"Do I need back-up?" Travis asked.

"No. Go in the parking lot then come around the far back. We're in the shadows."

"I'm on my way."

Max's panting got heavier. "You can't just keep me here. What do we do now?"

The knife was back at Max's throat. "We wait."

They waited.

Travis got there faster than he expected, having run into Home Depot. Jenny was examined and found to be fine with minimal blood loss. While Travis got Max into the backseat of his car, Stuart cleaned Jenny up and got her back in the bar with her friends. He begged off work with Mike for a family emergency and climbed in the passenger seat.

They drove by his bike, chained to the drain pipe as they headed home.

Everyone trickled in from their jobs while Travis and Stuart kept Max tied up in the kitchen. Tied with rope, duct tape on his mouth, he was attached to a chair by his wrists and ankles.

Jason came in from his room, glanced at Max then went for the coffee.

"We're out of milk," he said, pouring the last of it into his mug before adding sugar. "Do you know where Quinn is?"

Travis checked his watch. "Should be home any minute."

Jason took a sip and stared at the quiet Max.

"Good," he said. "I wanted to talk to him about something."

Stuart stared at the oak table, the knife still in his hand.

"No one was hurt," Travis said. Stuart's gaze jumped up.

"How do you know? He was in my bar on my watch and walked out with Jenny."

"Jenny Riley?" Jason snapped, standing straighter. "Is she okay?"

The front door shut, muffled voices could be heard as Quinn, having picked up Evan, came through to the kitchen.

They stopped to stare at the man tied to the chair.

Quinn sighed hard. He looked at Travis and raised the white gallon jug in his hand. "They were out of 'whole' so I had to go with '2%.'"

"That sucks," Jason moaned.

Quinn smiled at Travis. "Anything going on I should be aware of?"

Travis, his arms folded, shook his head. "Not that I can think of."

The chair started to bounce back and forth as Max rocked hard. He moaned and tried to speak past the tape. They let him ride the furniture.

"Is that human?" Evan asked, pointing at the noise.

"That tried to take a bite out of Jenny," Stuart said.

"Jenny Riley?" Quinn snapped. "Jenny's 5' 2" and weighs eighty pounds, if that. He bit her?" He looked to Travis. "Why is he alive?"

The noise turned into what sounded like a loud "no."

Stuart reached over and ripped the duct tape off. Max gasped and coughed.

"Oh, come on," he said. "What the fuck am I going to do here? Untie me."

"Shut up," Travis said, "or the tape goes back on."

"Are you sure?" Jason asked. "He looks kinda like a wuss."

"It was an accident," he said.

"An accident," Travis said. "You suggested Jenny out of the bar and chowed down and it's an accident?"

"When was the last time you ate?" Quinn asked.

"I don't know," he said.

"Does it have a name?" Evan asked.

"Hey," it snapped.

"Max. Its name is Max."

Quinn went to the refrigerator and pulled out a pitcher, he got a glass and came back, pouring.

"You know we need that," Evan pointed out.

Quinn put the glass to Max's lips. "You can drink or you can wear. Your choice."

"What is it?" Max asked, his voice cracking.

Quinn poured and Max only spat a little. It dribbled down his silk shirt and loosened tie.

"Do we have a plan for this?" Jason asked.

Travis looked to Stuart, then back. "We talked about it. We're thinking the bedroom is open downstairs."

"You want him to stay?" Evan asked. "He hurt Jenny."

"Do you even know Jenny?" Jason smirked.

"He hurt someone," Evan said. "We don't do that."

Quinn stepped back and Max was smacking his mouth.

"That stuff tastes like shit," Max said.

"Give it a couple of hours. The craving will start to diminish. It's what we use and we don't bite," Travis said.

"I don't want a room."

"Then you can go. Two of us will drive you far away. You can find a den or not, that's up to you. Just don't come back in this direction."

"Den's suck," Max said, looking at the floor. "Every move is watched and they butt into everything." He looked up at Travis. "You're Primary. What about Custodian and Slayer?"

"We don't have those," Travis said. "We're not traditional."

"What?" Max said.

"What's your story?" Travis asked.

"Same as yours. I was standing too close to someone once. Came back to bite me in the ass, so to speak."

"When?" Jason asked.

"1982. I'm thirty."

"Where?"

"Vancouver. I was working a bar—"

"You're a bartender?" Stuart asked.

He shook his head. "Not really. I've done it, but I suck." He laughed a little. "Suck at most things, I guess, even getting dinner without getting caught. Are you going to untie me?"

"You were turned in Vancouver, 1982?"

He nodded. "Yeah, I like it up there. It's pretty."

And that was the kind of thing that didn't make sense for him to say. Vampires didn't say things like that. They didn't notice things like 'pretty'. Getting their next meal was the only thing on their mind.

"So you're young?"

"You aren't? I mean, I know you're vampires." He nodded toward Stuart. "He showed to me."

"Most of us aren't young," Travis said.

"Will you untie me, please? It really hurts. I won't do anything, I promise."

They all exchanged glances, each silently weighing in.

Stuart grabbed the knife off the table and cut through the binding, the ropes falling in pieces to the floor.

"Woe," Max said, leaning forward, looking at the knife in Stuart's hand. "You're still going to kill me, though. Man," he said, shaking his head, "that really blows."

He didn't try to get up, get away or move. He slouched in acceptance at what he thought as his fate.

"Can I ask why five of you are living here? You're not a den but you're together."

"We're a den," Travis said. "We just redefined the Laws."

Max's gaze came up. "You can do that?"

"We live blood-free," Travis said. "That shit you just drank is called *Ace in the Hole*. Quinn makes it from a recipe he got in the fifties. It works."

"Who's Quinn."

Travis went around the room, giving the introductions.

"Blood-free?" He shook his head. "I don't believe you. Can't be done. No reason for it."

"Last victim I took was a bus driver named Jones, April 20, 1958."

Max stared at him, his mouth slightly agape. No words came out.

"All of us have similar stories and it's kinda pretty around here, too."

"I know," Max said hoarsely. "That's why I stopped here. I thought I might like it for a while."

"You stay here," Stuart said, "and I might cut your throat. When I see Jenny next, she better be in perfect shape."

"I didn't hurt her. Not much. I never do. I don't like killing them. I take enough to keep going and I give them a happy memory."

"You do what?" Jason laughed.

"Not that hard," Max said. "They're okay people so I think of something nice and leave them with that."

"How were you turned?" Jason asked.

"What? You can't ask me that. We don't ask that."

"Consider yourself asked," Travis said.

He struggled to find the words. "We don't do that."

"We do in this house," Travis said.

Max looked at Jason. "What about you? Are you going to tell me?"

"One night-stand gone wrong. Massachusetts, 1947."

Max looked at Travis. Travis didn't flinch or break eye contact. "Unexpected guest at my front door at 3:00 am. Bastard stuck around for a while."

Stuart smiled and looked up but didn't say anything.

"Girl I was dating," Max said, glancing up to Travis. "Went out with her a couple of times. It wasn't hard to get her into bed but I never thought there was anything weird about her. Then on our fourth date, we're in my room over the bar, sun-up about to happen and she tells me she likes me, wants to keep me around. Told me about these great friends I had to meet. It was over pretty quick, I guess. I don't remember much after that."

Travis took a step toward him. "We can offer you something here you will never find anywhere else. There is a free room downstairs. It's small and doesn't have any windows but it's clean and there's a bed."

"What are you saying?" Max asked.

Travis looked around, waiting for, and getting, the nods of everyone.

"We're saying if you want to do something different that keeps you out of situations like tonight, we'll teach you. We'll give you a place to stay. You find a job, settle in and we'll get you there."

Max lasted just over six months.

His jokes were as funny as Jason and Quinn's; Max's gaming score just about as high. Everyone wanted to play next round with him.

He got a job as a night clerk at a Mini Mart. The pay wasn't great, but he enjoyed it. He liked people, liked to make them laugh.

Then one day when he didn't show up for breakfast, Travis went to get him.

The room had been cleared of everything Max owned except for the naked woman half-conscious on his bed. The wound on her neck deep enough to require Quinn's attention. Blood stained the sheets near the pillow, a stark contrast to the white material. Her vacant eyes sat in a face too pale.

While Quinn bandaged, Travis looked around the room. On the small glass-topped table was a single piece of paper.

I'm sorry.

"What happened?" Travis asked, as she came back.

"I don't know," she smiled. "We were here and then he said he had to go. He kissed me and I fell asleep, I guess. He's going to come back, right?"

Quinn looked at Travis. Travis stared back.

"He told me about this nice bay, up north. It was pretty, he said. Just like the last time we were there."

Travis' gaze snapped up. "What?"

"When we went there together and skipped rocks at sunset. I don't think I was ever happier."

Yours, Mine and Ours
2008

Stuart read the face of his phone one more time.

Find me. Fast.

He put the phone in his back pocket.

"Nothing else," he said to Travis standing next to him at the back of the car, the trunk open. Travis reached in to pull out two scarves, handing one to Stuart.

"I'm thinking he might need two hands and ten fingers to send again," Travis said.

Evan hadn't come home. It had been enough hours for them to notice. The text was enough alert to get them moving.

Stuart pocketed his knife, pulled on fingerless gloves and saw Travis do the same. He reached up and slammed the trunk closed. They had layered under their coats with thermal tops, adding the mismatched scarves and splotches of dirt from the ground.

Travis stopped to look at Stuart. "You ready for this?"

"If I said no, what would you say?"

"Evan should have been home nine hours ago," Travis said.

"And we're going to get him back."

Stuart took a swig from the bottle of rum in his hand, laughing at nothing because that was their cover: homeless, drunk and lost was their ticket into that warehouse.

They had parked unseen in the distance by the shore, the smell of water obliterated by the rum. The warehouse loomed like a black apparition waiting for them to strike it down.

Moving toward it, Travis talked about dates he'd had and girls—all of which was the decoy to get them past the waiting crowd.

There were two black SUV's on the way to the white, cracked door. Both of them said money and more.

Evan was in there.

Evan had company.

And Evan's old friends weren't too thrilled with his new.

Stuart and Travis paused, looking at each other. It wasn't their first fight side by side. The quiet silence of encouragement lasted a few seconds. Long enough for Stuart to raise his eyebrows at Travis and take another swallow from the bottle.

Travis' laughter echoed around Stuart, making him smile as they went through the door, talking gibberish to throw off their targets.

No one touched Evan. He should be wearing a Handle With Care label that said just that.

"It doesn't matter," Travis said as they got close. He carried his own bottle in the brown bag in hand. "Chicks don't like the accent. You have to lose the accent."

"I don't have an accent," Stuart spoke, while scanning the hollow building.

Travis laughed as he looked to the left. "Trust me," Travis said. "You do."

The warehouse held old cars, smashed and stacked five high. It smelled of motor oil and mold. Behind them, light shone illuminating a tower of cars like a beacon.

Stuart moved right.

Travis, left.

"Wow," Stuart chuckled as the crowd came into view. He raised his finger, pointing. "People."

"No people here," Travis said. "This is our place."

Except there was a man watching them. Armed with something big and black and carrying too many rounds. He tracked their approach.

Another man—gun at the hip, a knife on the other hip. He held an automatic weapon in his hand. A third man was to the left fitting the same description.

"What are you doing here?" The Man snapped. His accent leaned toward educated English that didn't match the look of his leather and chains on his clothes.

"Us? This is our crib," Travis said. "Our rolls are up in the loft."

Evan, beaten bad, sat tied to a chair. Above him, an industrial sized skylight perfectly centered.

Evan didn't even look up as they arrived.

His hands were behind his back, his legs tied down. A piece of duct tape covered his mouth. The ash white look of his face showed under the blood smears and bruises. Two bullet holes were on his chest with a knife slash on his neck. He listed to the left and it seemed as if he was struggling to even stay conscious.

His phone lay in pieces under his chair.

"That's a kid," Stuart snapped. "You can't do that to a kid."

"What the fuck are you doing in here?" The Man asked confused.

Stuart pointed to the chair. "You have a kid in here," he said again. "You can't have a kid in here. This is our house."

"This looks like a kid?" the man grinned. "He fools you, doesn't he?"

Stuart felt his fingers tighten on his bottle. Fury ate at him when he still had to pretend. In his own mind, Stuart knew whoever this was, they were dying tonight.

"That's a lot of blood," Travis said. "Why is there so much blood?"

"Because that's what he wants," The Man said. "Gallons of it."

"Who the hell are you?" Travis barked.

"Don't think it's really any of your business, but I would run along and sleep where you want. I've got work to do here."

"Think of another plan," Travis said.

"Why would I do that for a couple drunks? Jensen, search them."

The other man moved with deliberation, but it wasn't enough. Travis stepped forward. "Gun or not, that is the second worse plan I've heard."

The other man, staring into Travis' face. Without Travis 'showing' his expression said enough. He stood to his full height—former dock worker written in his stance and expression

Before Stuart could move The Man had a gun on Evan's head. Stuart held back and hated him even more.

"He looks like a kid."

"You see these holes, The Man said. "I shot him, but he keeps on breathing. You know any kid who can do that?"

"This is our house," Travis repeated, taking a drink off his bottle. "Our beds are here. We sleep here." He looked at Stuart. "This is where we left the rolls, right?"

"He's a Goddamn kid," Stuart said, seething. "You need this kind of force against a kid?"

"That's not a fucking kid. How old is he? A hundred? Two hundred?"

"Looks seventeen," Travis said.

Shots fired in the backyard, the sounds muffled by the steel walls. Everyone stared at the faded and barely working door.

"I don't like vampires," The Man said. He nodded at the to the other guy. "Check."

"Are you out of your mind? Vampi—" Stuart snapped.

151

"Who's out back?" Travis asked.

"I imagine," The Man said, "Some of your guys are dead."

His men moved toward the door.

"I know our guys," Travis said, giving up the pretense. "They wouldn't be the ones going down."

On cue, the door flew back on its hinge. Quinn came in high, Jason low.

The two guards tried to rise in time, but were too slow. Quinn and Jason fired first, hitting both targets.

Blood splattered the floor. The smell of gun powder circled their heads.

"That would be our guys," Travis said. "Want to step back from my baby brother?"

The man shifted, pushing the gun flush with Evan's head. The Man's stare was ice cold, his hands steady. He would kill Evan.

"No," Stuart snapped, jumping two feet closer, his hands out. "He's not what you think."

The Man looked back to Stuart. "That's interesting. What is he?"

"He's...different."

"We didn't have guns," Travis said to Jason.

"But his people did," Jason smiled, holding one up, hanging on his finger. "Since they didn't need them anymore we decided to even the field."

Quinn moved over to the man moaning on the floor. He fired three shots into and across the bastard's throat with the precision of someone who already knew how to use the gun.

The man fizzled and quivered, his whole body convulsing into dust.

Vampires burst into ash.

Humans, not so much.

Stuart knew. Killing was this vampire's hobby, one that didn't let victims live to walk away. Here and now, they terrorized Evan, which fit the mold. If let standing, they would kill again.

That was reason enough to take them down.

Hurting Evan secured the warrant for their deaths.

"Fuck," Stuart whispered. "You're fucking vampires? And you did this to him?"

"The two guys in the back, too," Quinn said.

"Looked like they knew what they were doing," Jason said. He copied Quinn, firing into the neck of the other fallen.

"You're a fucking vampire?" Travis asked again, moving closer.

"I hate vampires." The Vampire spat.

Travis coughed out a half tired laugh. "Get the fuck away from my brother."

The Vampire looked at the ground, the gun still against Evan's head. "You're his damn den. I didn't know he had a den."

Which was stupid. Just about every vampire had one.

Stuart stepped forward. "The sun will be up in minutes. Unless you want this to end different, back away."

"He's already dead," Quinn said in a calm voice, pointing out his argument with limited vocabulary.

The Vampire took a step back and glanced at the ceiling above. "You want to take off? The sun's coming up."

"Tell me why a vampire would do this to one of their own?" Stuart demanded.

"We're done," The Vampire said, looking at Stuart. "Take him, get out. I won't come looking for you."

"Your men?" Travis asked.

"Expendable."

Quinn looked at Evan, then The Vampire. "He was going to be your dinner."

"As far as I'm concerned, it's the only use for a blood sucking bastard."

"Hey," Stuart snapped. "Why?" The Vampire looked at him, Stuart had his attention. The gun slipped off Evan's temple.

The Man smiled like it was a joke. "He's prey. I'm not." He drew the word out ending on a hiss. Travis glared at him.

"Humans are easy," he said. "Vampires make the fight worth it. And him, it was exceptional seeing what he could take."

Stuart saw Jason and Quinn exchange a silent look. The guns came up. Shots fired, directly into The Vampire. As the clips emptied, holes appeared in The Vampire. Blood poured, sending him onto the ground He pushed, trying to right himself. He looked to one pile of ash, then the other.

"Don't like…fucking…vampires." He gasped, then pushed himself up.

Law IV. *To disobey is to call for your own death by your own kind.*

Quinn and Jason did enough damage. When Travis grabbed the edge of the chair to pull Evan away from the skylight, Stuart helped. Quinn and Jason each grabbed a leg and pulled The Man into the spot, right below the skylight.

Above, the skylight burst with color and light, showering down on them. The Man tried to crawl, tried to move. Only a vampire could take that kind of damage and keep going. Jason took one side of the circle of light. Quinn the other. They blocked his escape.

Stuart looked up, feeling the sunshine on his face in ways he hadn't in decades. Closing his eyes, he heard The Vampire's screams, high pitched and uncontrolled. By the time Stuart looked, The Man glowed in the orange flames, rolling on the ground, a victim of the sun, that didn't hurt the others. Nanette's tattoos' promise fulfilled.

"They jumped me," Evan panted as Quinn cut through the ropes. "By the park."

"You okay?" Jason asked.

Evan only managed to get one side of his mouth to smile. "Maybe."

Quinn stood up from examining him. "You're sorta fucked up," he said.

Evan almost laughed. He still listed to the left but there seemed to be a light in him that for a moment was gone.

"Can we stop and get dinner on the way home?" Evan asked.

Stuart smiled at him and rubbed his shoulder. "Only if they have a drive through."

Late Good-byes
2013

Usually time spent at work was pretty good. Tonight, not so much. Carrying his bike up the stairs an hour later than he normally would, Stuart got the door open and parked it by the basement door.

He was tired, irritated and just wanted a couple of beers and the Tom Clancy he was reading in his attic room.

Going to the kitchen by way of the dining room, he saw the TV on and the back of Travis' head. With the refrigerator already open, he reached in, pulled out the beer and watched the family room from where he stood.

The *Bourne Identity* played, and it was far enough along to say Travis had been there a while.

Moving closer to the pass-through, Stuart twisted off the cap.

"What are you doing?" he asked.

"Nothing."

"Thought you had work tonight."

Stuart heard a loud intake of breath, followed by a sigh.

"Apparently, I'm home."

Travis picked up the remote and upped the volume, signaling an end to the conversation.

Stuart tossed his lid into the sink and decided the book upstairs could wait.

Going into the room, Stuart stood behind the couch; saw Jason Bourne on the big screen and two bottles of Bacardi 151 on the coffee table. One was empty. One was on its way there. The glass at Travis' lips held a healthy portion.

Stuart took a drink from the beer and felt Travis' pain hang in the family room like a livewire of energy, sparking the air.

"Anyone else home?" Stuart asked.

"No." The voice was clipped, hard and totally out of line for anything the Master of Muddling could create.

"You going to tell me what's going on?" Stuart asked.

"If you want to grab another bottle and a glass, that's fine. Otherwise shut the fuck up, sit down and watch the fucking movie."

"*Okaaaay,*" Stuart smiled. The anticipation of the quiet night at home melted away.

By the time *The Bourne Supremacy* started, Jason had come in from the gym. He walked silently through, repeating the same actions as Stuart, watching from the pass-through, too.

With his beer bottle, he came in and looked at Stuart who shrugged. Jason used his finger to silently count the bottles of Bacardi—now three—before looking hard at Stuart.

Stuart pointed at Travis.

Jason came closer to the couch, talking to Travis, "It's kinda late for Part II. You planning on heading into Part III tonight?"

"Bite me, Irishman," Travis said.

Stuart watched Jason narrow enough to move his eyebrows. Jason went to the stools to sit back to watch.

Quinn came in next. He didn't get to the kitchen, Stuart noted. He stopped in front of Jason and..

"What?" Quinn asked. "It was a long night so just what?"

Jason pointed to the couch.

Stuart saw Quinn walk to the back of the couch, look at the bottles, pursed his lips and he cocked his head, then looked at Travis, leaning over to talk to him.

"Hey, how was your night?" Quinn smiled.

"My night was fuck you," Travis snapped. "Any more questions?" Travis leaned forward to the bottle.

"Do anything interesting today?" Stuart tried with a smile.

Travis didn't even look at him.

Evan walked in, looking tired. He stopped to look at Jason and Quinn at the pass-through. Quinn nodded toward the couch and Evan's gaze followed. Stuart stayed stretched out, but returned the look.

Evan looked back and both Quinn and Jason shrugged.

"Oh, fuck that," Evan said. He turned around, headed to the couch to stand next to Travis. Travis watched the movie without looking up.

"You drunk?" Evan asked him. When Travis ignored him, Evan kicked him in the foot.

Travis looked up. "What do you want?"

Evan glared at him. "My night sucked. I'm supposed to come home to get over that. Not walk into more. You got a problem, we got a problem so get off your pity party and talk."

Evan rarely said a hard word. No one said one back to him now.

Travis stared at him, cocking his head then said. "Have a drink. It helps."

"What does it help?" Evan asked.

Stuart saw more concern than annoyance in the kid.

Travis turned the movie to mute and stared up at Evan. Bourne kept moving on the screen.

"Shelly Connors is dead," he said, taking a long drink, emptying the glass. He learned over and poured more.

Stuart sat up, his feet on the floor. "What?"

Travis leaned back on the couch and stared into his glass.

"She died July 28, 1998, six months after she left us."

Jason and Quinn came closer.

Stuart stared at Travis and felt the pain. Shelly had been a part of them for almost ten months, privy to their secret but never telling. She shared Travis' bedroom and when he offered her a lifetime, she thought long and hard before saying no, breaking all their hearts.

She just about killed Travis. He had loved her more than anything.

"She left here and died?" Evan whispered. "She was supposed to tackle the world."

Travis nodded and drank. "She walked out the door on December 29, 1997 and missed our outstanding New Year's Party that year."

There hadn't been a party. There rarely was.

Stuart saw Jason head to the liquor cabinet. Quinn went for the glasses.

"What happened?"

"I don't know why I was Googling her. I never had before. She had an accident on her bike. The article said she was in traffic. And on this occasion, she wasn't wearing her helmet."

"She always wore her helmet," Stuart said. "She tried to get me to wear one."

Stuart learned his love of biking from Shelly. Travis never had a problem when Stuart and she took off for mile long rides.

"She's buried in Hollywood Memorial Gardens. I couldn't find any photos of the funeral, but there's a nice shot of her name on a photo of a plaque on Find-A-Grave."

Jason sat down, Quinn beside him. Evan sat by Stuart. Quinn handed out the glasses, Jason cracked the seal on two more 151's.

"Do you want me to look?" Jason asked. "I might be able to dig something up."

Travis shook his head. "No. I thought of that. I don't need to see her like that."

Shelly Conners had been the one true love of Travis Ricci. He would have gone to hell and back for her.

"Man," Jason said, breaking the long silence of their drink. "Chick could tune your engine."

Even Travis laughed, though it looked as if it hurt.

"You had to find the only 36-24-36 D Cup mechanic in the area," Quinn chuckled.

Travis sat up. "She was not—and you shouldn't notice anyway," he blubbered. "Okay, she was close."

"She lived with us and you think that might slip past us?"

"Because they were always so quiet when they were in their room," Evan said, getting a couch pillow launched at his head.

"She kept all of our cars running while looking great doing it," Stuart said. "Was never really sure how you pulled that one off."

"I found the only auto mechanic in the Pacific Northwest who could rip apart an engine, get covered in grease and still look great in black pumps."

"As long as you kept her in the garage," Quinn said. "Bring her in the kitchen and the smoke detectors went off."

"Travis, were you aware your girlfriend couldn't cook to save her life?"

He closed his eyes tight. "And I had to eat all of it with a smile."

They laughed.

"Remember those cookies?" Jason asked.

Travis looked at him. "Those were Christmas ornaments. You ate them before she could paint them."

"Not all of them," Jason laughed.

"Pancakes," Quinn said.

"Chocolate cake with that…" Stuart motioned with his finger in a circle. "That stuff on it. What was that?"

Travis looked at him. "Icing."

"That was icing?"

Jason left and came back five minutes later. "I checked the computer," he said. "Hollywood Memorial Gardens is one of the cemeteries in the area that is open at nights. Find-A-Grave had the location of her grave."

Travis shifted his gaze to him.

Jason shrugged a shoulder. "I can be ready in ten minutes. It's about fifteen hour drive so we have to break it up due to daylight hours but my Tahoe holds all of us comfortably and we can probably call a florist in the area to stay open for us."

Travis stared at him with a drunken gaze. "You want to drive to LA tonight, go to the cemetery and…what?"

"I want to go and give a last good-bye to someone I thought of as a friend. Is that something you think you want to do, since she never had a room of her own?"

"I'll have to call the vet," Evan said.

Quinn shrugged. "I can claim a death in the family. Have to go. They won't argue." He headed toward the phone.

Stuart stared at Travis without a worry. Mike would be easy, he knew. Stuart was worried more about Travis.

Shelly had chosen to leave when Travis offered her a chance to be like them. He knew he was never going to see her again. He knew that one day she would pass and he would continue to go on into the next century. Stuart had the distinct feeling Travis had wanted to go toward old, grey and grandkids.

Gone six months after she left. Stuart doubted she was even dating yet.

Jason turned to head up the stairs. Quinn and Evan followed.

Stuart stayed on the couch staring at Travis, who watched the coffee table.

"Will it make it harder or easier?"

Travis looked at him. "If I had made a different decision..."

"If you had forced our life on her when she wanted to go back to LA? You think that would have been a good idea?"

"She would be alive. She would have been here with me instead of in the ground."

Stuart sat forward and chose his words carefully. Grief was an angry monster who breathed in sorrow. Stuart didn't want to add more.

"She spent almost a week agonizing over it. All that time you asked. She trusted all of us not to do that to her. Travis, I think when she made the decision she did, she knew what it meant and she knew what she lost."

"She's been dead seventeen years, Stuart. That is seventeen years she could have been keeping me warm."

"You know what I always envied you for?"

Travis looked at him.

"The way she looked at you. You didn't have to try that hard to win her over and she looked at you like you mattered. She was in love with you from Day One. It's just not a lifestyle she could do forever."

"I did the right thing."

Stuart noted the statement and not the question. "You gave her a choice. Something all of us wish we had had. Would we have decided to take the change? I don't know. I just know you asking and not forcing was the best thing for her and for you."

"I hate your fucking guts. You know that, right?"

Stuart smiled. "Aye, I know."

Driving through the night, they made to Sacramento and got a couple of rooms in a Ramada to wait out the day. The next night, they made it to Palmdale where they got rooms again and a phone to find a florist in the San Fernando Valley who would work with them.

Roses were ordered.

Red ones.

As many as they could take.

The next night they drove into the Hollywood Hills to find the gate.

Jason had enough information to navigate the roads in the limited light, getting them to an area of the cemetery not too far from the section marked 'devotion'.

Rochelle Anna Connors

May 1, 1968 – July 28, 1998

And underneath, centered to stand out:

fiends goblins beasts

"I never stopped loving you. I always missed you..." ~Shelly

dc

Travis knelt down to run his fingers over the letters, coming to stop on top of the initials.

"Who's dc?" Stuart asked.

"My guess? Danielle—Shelly's baby sister. Shelly must have said something." He looked up at Stuart. "She would have told Danielle. Danielle would have believed her."

"She left this for you to find. She wanted you to know."

He stood up. "Yeah, I guess."

Evan put the four pillar candles in the four corners of the oversized plaque, lighting them.

The five sat down on the damp grass, Travis facing the name, and they began to remember. The moon hid behind clouds, casting a dark shadow over the area. The quiet of death hung low tonight, eerie even for vampires.

She gave each one of us a birthday party without ever touching a stove or oven. Take-in and bakeries were good.

She fixed every broken down part on each of our cars refusing compensation.

She played poker like one of us, bluffing us out of hands and rarely gloating.

She always smelled good.

Travis' gaze shifted to Jason's.

"What?" Jason smiled. "She did and I never could figure out what the perfume was."

Travis looked at her name and smiled a little. "She didn't wear perfume. She used essential oils on pulse points."

Jason smiled more. Then he sighed. *"From a sudden and unprovoked death, deliver us, O Lord."*

Jason had raised been Catholic. Stuart and Travis, too. The blessing for the dead was appreciated.

"Amen," Travis said.

It wasn't Shelly's birthday quite yet. That is the day Danielle would normally visit. Though, today she took a break from her job at Burbank Studios and drove the distance into the cemetery. Shelly had been with her all day, trying to say something Danielle couldn't figure out. Danielle wasn't one who normally believed in the supernatural, but she trusted her judgment when big sister wanted to be heard.

There was a need today. A feeling she couldn't explain to herself or anyone.

Parking her Lexus on the drive, she walked past the names on plaques of people she had memorized ages ago.

Her big sister had been her idol. Losing her had just about killed Danielle.

As she walked closer to the spot, she slowed her steps, looking at the site.

Roses. Dozens and dozens of them, all over the plaque that marked the grave. Air caught in Danielle's lungs. She put her hand to her gut to still the exhilaration. The list of who would have done this last night was so short she couldn't focus.

Moving closer, she saw the burned out candles, her sister's name obliterated by flowers which hadn't even started to wilt.

At the bottom, near the secret message she had added to the plaque was a small piece of paper, held in place by candle wax.

She was one of a kind. We miss her.

Thank you for understanding that.

It was signed in five different hands, in a variety of places on the paper.

T. S. Q. J. E

They came at night with no fanfare or expressions to the excess. Danielle stared down at the note, a tear on her face. When Shelly had told her about her friends, Danielle had not believed. But it had been Shelly's last wish in the hospital that Danielle tell him, tell him she was sorry. Danielle searched

Shelly's apartment, her car, everywhere, but there had been no contact information. No last name.

Danielle had done the only thing she could think of to reach him.

She made her sister's last wish come true, that he knew Shelly still cared.

She looked at the piles of roses, her sister's name visible. "You were right, Shelly" she whispered. "He was worth it.

My Sheets Are Blue
2013

The door opened, he paused.

She turned to look at him.

"Aren't you going to come in?" she asked.

He smiled. "Thanks."

With his hands in his pockets, he glanced around, nodding in approval at the decoration, the art on the walls. "Nice," he said. "Roger didn't like it?" He grinned.

An image of her ex jumped into her mind as fast as it jumped out. "Roger never had the chance to see it."

"He wasn't curious?" he asked as he walked around, looking at the art on her walls.

"He wasn't offered the opportunity."

He nodded and headed down the hall.

"Bathroom is through the master," she said.

She got two crystal glasses and a bottle of Macallan.

The shower went on, piquing her curiosity. She poured them each a portion then screwed the cap back on, leaving the bottle on the counter near the dishes she had planned on doing later.

"Found the bathroom?" she teased.

"Was checking out the sheets. They *are* blue."

"I told you," she smiled.

"I believe you." His accent thickened, upping his hot status.

He held up the glass between them, waiting, his gaze locked on hers.

She lifted hers, but didn't follow through on the toast.

He rolled the glass back and forth. He looked up. "We have an understanding on the rules?"

"There are rules?"

"I will never ask you about who came before," he said. "And I won't offer who I was with."

"You don't have to make promises," she smiled, shyly.

He set the glass down. "Then I don't need to be here, Ashley."

The comment came unexpected and her gut heaved and dropped. She stared at the counter.

Leaving his glass the counter, he came around. She turned as he stepped right to her.

All bravado deserted her when confronted with him this close while she thought of sex. She took a deep breath then exhaled slow. She stared at his chest while reaching up to play with the first button of his plaid shirt. It slipped open in her fingers.

He didn't say stop.

"Take a drink," he said.

She looked up at him. "Right now?"

"Aye," he said. "We can settle this quick. Macallan is my favorite scotch and yours is eighteen years old. I think I want to make sure you and the scotch go together. Take a drink."

She looked at the glass next to her. Wrapping her fingers around it, she sipped the smooth heat.

He took the glass away from her, setting it aside. Leaning in, he covered her mouth with his and snaked his hand around her waist to pull her to him. Her whole body pressed against a hard chest. Focus was impossible. His lips or his hands, everything he did to her, sent waves of electric shock to every one of her nerve endings.

He shifted with a muffled moan. His mouth hard and wide, taking what he wanted while giving back just as much. He took his time to learn her mood, to adjust according to what she wanted, all the while bordering on wild. His fingers fisted in her hair.

When he stopped, he held her face, his eyes closed. "*Wooww,*" he sighed.

"Well?" she grinned, biting her lip, looking up at him.

"You and Macallan mix just fine." His voice was breathless.

"I have Jamison, if you want to double check."

"I think we're good," he smiled, trailing a finger down her cheek.

"A shower?" she asked. Another of his buttons fell apart. Then the next. Each one made her more bolder. She pushed her fingers into the material at his shoulders, letting the shirt fall to the floor.

He looked at her, leaning in, staring at her mouth as if he wanted more.

"I'm going to wash your hair."

"Are you?"

"I'm going to wash your hair, then soap you up clean so you can pick out your favorite pajamas. Then I'm going to peel you out of them."

She sighed instead of answering him.

"You understand the rules?" he asked.

She looked up at him.

"Exclusive rights are mine. Until we decide otherwise, it's only you and me in this relationship."

With his hand on her lower back, he pulled her close. He smiled then he shrugged out of the T-shirt underneath the outer shirt.Half naked and totally incredible. Her mouth went dry and she moved her hands over his skin. She had known he was hot but she hadn't a clue he had this body under the shirts. A gym was on his daily routine. Maybe more than the gym. He had a sprinkling of dark hair. The tattoo armband on his left bicep was a surprise, but then, so was how much she liked it. A mixture of swirls and circles, it was most definitely Celtic in design to match the accent.

"I like hot water," he said, "but I don't want to scald you if you're not used to it. Is that all right?"

"You're serious?" she said again, this time in a lower voice.

He leaned over to whisper in her ear. "Do you want to get out of those clothes on your own, or do you need help?" He brushed a gentle kiss across her lips.

The grin alone was killing her.

Later, he rolled away, cleaned up and crawled under the blankets. She watched him without joining him.

"What?" he asked.

"You do know that sex wakes women up as much as it puts men to sleep?"

He laughed harder than he had all night. "Okay, what am I supposed to do with you now?"

She shrugged and smiled. "You go to sleep. I'll watch you."

"It's three-thirty in the morning. How about you crawl under the covers, we turn off the lights and we close our eyes to see what happens."

"You'll fall asleep."

He braced up on his elbows and huffed. "I'm still one up on you."

She eyed him. "What's that supposed to mean?"

"We don't want to start off our relationship with things uneven. I should probably do something about that whole evil shower routine."

She smiled wickedly. On her knees in front of him in the shower was as good for her as him. She laughed and tried to dart when he pinned her under him, his hands grabbing her wrists and holding them over her head. She wiggled and squirmed.

"What?" she laughed.

"Where is it?"

"Where is what?"

"Your vibrator."

"What?" She laughed, straining to get away but he was too big and too strong to budge and if the truth be known, even after astronomical sex, it felt right where he was still all naked.

"I am not answering that question," she laughed.

"There is a vibrator nearby. I'll just have to tie you down and search for it myself. Only a few places you would put it."

And he thought it was a threat that would scare her? "I don't admit to having one."

He smiled and nodded his head slowly. "Right or left side of the bed?"

She worked her jaw. "Right side. Near the headboard."

He kissed her, a brushing of lips. "Now answer one question and I will finish off this night with a bang so we can get some sleep."

"It's purple."

He laughed again. "I think I'm in love with you. Is that a problem?"

"We can work around it. What's your question?"

"Last night, after we spoke, did you come back here and use it?"

She felt the blush hit her cheeks and saw his grin spread even wider. She laughed and squirmed under his direct gaze.

"Do you have any idea how hot that is?" he asked.

He settled further onto her, redistributing his weight to make her feel him all over. Her hands were still over her head, his face so damn close to hers.

"Did you say my name?" he asked.

"I thought you wanted to sleep."

"I think you woke me up with the color coding. Did you say it? Say my name out loud in the dark in this bed when it was only you?" He kissed along her neck. Beautiful, warm, wet kisses taking her already satisfied body and bringing new life to it.

"If I say no you're going to be very disappointment, aren't you?"

"No. But I am also going to know you're lying." He laughed when she pulled her hands down.

She laughed hard. "It's the accent. I like accents."

"That's the whole story, huh?"

"You going to kiss me again?"

"Haven't you been kissed enough for one night?"

She pulled a hand back, ran her finger along his jaw. She would swear they had been at this long enough for his five o'clock shadow to get thicker.

"I seriously don't think I could ever get enough of you kissing me." She looked right into his eyes and saw the desire where there should be exhaustion.

He smiled and lowered his head to give her one long, moist and meaningful one. She trembled in his arms and never wanted to be anywhere else.

He shifted off her, reaching between the mattress and box spring, coming back quick to lie down beside her, his whole body pressed up against hers like a warm extended caress. She pushed back, giving him the same.

He leaned so he spoke directly into her ear, his breath moving her hair. "You're going to talk me through this, tell me what you like, what feels good?"

"You can't figure it out?"

"I am sure I could, but I like to hear your words."

She leaned her head back. "Why do I get the feeling that before we are done here, you're still going to be one up on me?"

He looked at the nightstand. "That's a big box of condoms."

She smiled at him, putting her arms over her head and stretching.

He picked up her toy, laughed sexily, held up his prize in his hand and dramatically turned it on. "Close your eyes, relax and see if maybe you can enjoy this. I'll even say your name in your ear and lay the accent on thick."

Rachel and Sarah
2016

Empty beer bottle in hand, Jason waited until they were all the way into the family room. Ash slept on the couch. Jason reached up from his chair and turned on the lamp beside him.

They jumped and turned quick, the wide-eyed look of shock replaced by guilt in a heartbeat. Sarah stood in front, dressed to travel. She had a blade in her hand, a six inch razor-sharp bone-handle piece of art. A person who knew knives carried blades like this.

She stood three feet from Ash, six from Jason. He was confident he could get to Ash in time.

"Nice knife," he said.

"Girl's got to be careful," Sarah said.

"Yeah," he said, "Especially around here because we've always been so hostile."

"Actually," she said, "for the first few months we were here, it wasn't so bad. You're all pretty nice to look at and we got to do some role playing. We liked all the attention. Even your bitch tried to help us out."

"My bitch's name is Ashley. I would prefer you call her that."

"Whatever," Sarah smiled.

Jason watched Sarah. "And you lied to us after we welcomed you in?"

"We're vampires. You expect us to follow rules?"

"We're vampires. We do."

"You're not vampires," Sarah snapped. "You stopped the day you gave up your heritage. You're not human, either so I just don't know what that makes you except kind of pathetic."

"You've been taking victims," Jason said.

"So?" she laughed.

"Who turned Travis?" Rachel asked. "It had to be someone in that room or Ashley would have given up a name today."

"Does it matter?"

"You're going to be dead soon," Sarah said. "So not really. We were just wondering."

"It was Stuart."

Rachael slapped Sarah on the back. "I told you."

"I thought it was the Doctor."

"Doctor has a name," Jason said.

"Yeah, but apparently he doesn't have a real love life," Rachel said. "I didn't know why before. He was always so sad and seemed distracted. I thought it was about Ashley. Still, he's a lot of fun to roll with."

"I'll tell him you said that," Jason said.

"From what we can tell from the bullshit your toy was spewing? The one thing she did get right was all of you are dynamite in bed."

Jason grinned mean. "My toy's name is Ashley," he said again. "She's real sick. And that would be hard for you to know since you didn't sleep with all of us. I think Quinn would have told me if he was sleeping with Sarah."

"Why would he mention it if he was enjoying it so much?" Sarah asked.

Jason shook his head. "You really don't know people, do you?"

She pointed the knife at Ash. "Well, I know I'm tired of talking to you because talking to you always did bore me. And I'm tired of her. She controls every one of you like you're her pets. Drain cleaner didn't work, so let's see what does."

"Drain cleaner?"

Rachel laughed. "We tried drain cleaner. Pine Sol. Antifreeze. We thought that would do something. Always worked on TV, but I guess she's not as human as we thought."

"You were feeding her antifreeze?"

"What are you worried about? It didn't work. And now, I am going to slice her throat deep enough to count. You can watch me do it and then I'll kill you, or I can kill you first and you can die knowing you couldn't save her."

"I think your plans suck," Jason said.

"Well yeah, but it's my plan so I get to make the rules."

"Can you even comprehend what is going to happen to you if you lay a hand on her?"

"Give it up. There's not going to be any heartfelt changes here. This is over and you're leaving town in a way no one will ever know."

"You really think this den is going to think I just walked out one day after fifty years?"

"She'll be gone, too, so they'll probably think you left together. The way you two play, no one would doubt it."

"You're that good?" Jason asked.

"Jason, I am so fucking good, I doubt you will even feel it."

"I know a guy like that, too. Amazing to watch with a knife and they never see it coming. He's really cool. Have a lot of respect for him."

"Maybe you should introduce us sometime."

"You know she named us," Jason said. "Ages ago."

"Give it up, Jason. In about two minutes your precious Ash is going to be dust and she is so stoned thanks to the doctor friend of yours, she won't know it."

"I knew you were a bitch the first night I met you. I'm ashamed I didn't realize you were a homicidal psychopath."

She smiled again.

"Ash picked a personality trait out for each of us and gave us a nickname that stuck. The Protector, Scotsman, Kid, Genius and Flirt. Want to guess which is my tag?"

"I don't really give a shit, but I'll go with Flirt."

"No," a voice said behind them, making the girls spin. Quinn stood in the corner, waving his own blade open in his hand like a salutation. Not as long a piece. Not as wide, but looking so much more deadly with the man behind it.

"I'm The Flirt. You've been here for three months and you never knew that. Also why on earth, Sarah, would you ever think I would sleep with Rachel's leftovers?"

Jason started talking. "I was the Genius because, if you hadn't noticed, I can think off the charts and the one thing a genius is not going to do is wait in a dark room alone for two lunatics. Sarah, you wanted to meet my knife friend," he pointed. "This is Quinn Nelson. Best I ever saw with a blade. And Rachel, sorry to say, but as good as he is, I do think you are going to see it coming."

"I don't like liars," Quinn said, "I don't like threats against ours and I really don't like you."

"It was talk," Rachel said. "Just talk. We were just going to go and not bother you again."

She started to move toward the door.

"No," Sarah said. "We finish this."

"We can't finish this," Rachel said. "You're good, I know. But I have a feeling he is better."

Sarah stood her ground.

"Jason," Quinn said.

"What?"

"Did you ever stop to think that once a vampire has been invited into a house, you can't undo the invite?"

"No," Jason said. "I hadn't thought of that, but I can see why it could be a problem for us."

"No," Quinn sighed. "It's not going to be a problem."

"Quinn," Rachel said, "Please. We had fun. We had a lot of fun. I can do that again. Those things you like. Remember?"

"I remember you just told us, not even threatened, you *told* us you were planning on killing Ashley. Do you have any idea how much more weight that is going to carry?"

Rachel lunged at Quinn fast and sharp. But he came forward and Jason saw him grab her, spinning her around with a yelp to slam her into the wall. He covered her mouth with his hand, muffling her cry and the blade flashed.

A split second later Sarah leapt toward Jason, knife ready. Jason dropped the bottle and came out of the chair without a weapon.

She got two slices off, catching him in the forearm deep and in the side deeper. Human and it would be fatal. Vampire and he was just pissed. He got her by the shoulders, spun her, capturing her around the face, his hand on her chin, pulling her back against his body. With her pinned and control of the hand that held the knife, he raised it up fast and stopped, hesitating.

"Jason, don't," she whimpered. "Please…"

He closed his eyes and spoke into her ear. "I'm sorry."

He brought the hand and blade up, his eyes closed tight. She was a blood-sucking psycho but it didn't mean it didn't hurt to be the one to do it.

She vanished in his arms, her body disappearing in a rain of ash that fell slowly to the floor. The only thing left was the blade that dropped and pinged as it hit the hard wood.

"Let me see," Quinn said. Jason opened his eyes and saw Quinn reaching for him.

"Look at your arm," Quinn said.

Jason looked down and saw the rip in his shirt, the blood pouring out.

"Your side, too."

Quinn lifted the shirt to poke at the slice. "Damn she was good. In another life, this one might have killed you. You're going to need a shitload of stitches."

"What do you think?" Jason said.

Quinn choked out a hard humorless laugh. "I think my taste in women sucks."

Jason bobbed his head. "Well, yeah," he said, trying to smile. "But she had really nice boobs. Real round and perky," he said, using his hands for emphasis.

Quinn laughed.

Travis sat a plate down in front of Ash. "French toast, maple syrup," he leaned over and sprinkled onto the plate. "Powdered sugar." He smiled.

"Thank you," she beamed, reaching for her fork.

"Where's mine?" Stuart asked.

"Make it yourself."

"You're a bastard and you know it."

"Everything is out on the counter and I mixed plenty. Knock yourself out."

Stuart picked up his fork and tried to stab at her breakfast but she batted him away with her fork while she laughed.

"What were you doing this morning?" Stuart asked as he snaked a piece.

"With what?" Travis asked.

"The noise."

"Vacuuming."

"It's not Saturday."

Travis leaned back against the counter and folded his arms over his chest. "There was something spilled in the family room and a mark on the wall I had to scrub off."

Jason and Quinn drank their coffee and stared at each other without a word.

"What?"

"I don't know what either was. Stuff on the wall was a bitch to get off and the stuff on the ground was sort of dirty looking. Looked like someone had tried to sweep it up but they did a terrible job. There was enough left that I had to get it before the neat freak found it. Weird, too. It was in two different spots. In front of the chair near the couch and over by the wall next to the TV."

Stuart looked at him then at Jason and Quinn.

"Trying to figure out what to do with the bag, though," Travis said.

"What?" Stuart asked.

"The bag. The vacuum bag. I was thinking I should do something with it."

"Garbage," Quinn and Jason said together.

"I had a feeling you two were going to say that," Travis said.

Evan came in.

"They're gone," Evan said. "I went to Rachel and Sarah's rooms. Their beds haven't been slept in but all their stuff is still here and their suitcases are in the closets. Looks like they went light."

He looked at Quinn and Jason. Stuart watched them, too. Neither of them would look up.

"They left because of me," Ash said.

"No," Jason said, snapping his head up to look at her. "They left because of themselves."

Travis cleared the last of the dishes, put the soap in the dishwasher and closed it.

When he stepped back, Jason was beside him.

"You getting sneaky?"

Jason set a micro cassette recorder, complete with headphones on the counter beside Travis.

Travis looked at it then at Jason.

"It's obvious you know. We weren't going to say anything and hoped no one noticed and just thought they left as instructed. We talked about it and don't want to start secrets."

"So what is this?"

"I knew they were dangerous. If we were lost and disappeared and had to be vacuumed up, we wanted to make sure you or Stuart found this and knew what happened so you could protect Ash. I had it by the TV the whole time. I listened to it already. It recorded the whole thing."

Travis stared at it. "Is listening to it going to upset me?"

"Beyond your wildest imagination."

An hour later, Travis found Stuart on the back in a chair, staring off into space with a cup of coffee in his hand.

"So, whatcha doin'?" Travis smiled.

Stuart looked up at him like he was seeing him for the first time. "Oh, um. Ash is passed out upstairs. I thought I would take a few minutes to decompress."

"Quinn says she's going to be fine."

"I know," Stuart said. "I still worry."

"Twenty-four hours ago a hell of a lot of shit went down in this house. How long had Rachel been hitting on you?"

Stuart's gaze came up.

"She started the day they walked in. I thought if I'd ignore it, let her know I was with Ash, it would stop." He looked at Travis. "She never did. They were going to kill Ash for it, too. That's twisted."

"Yes they were. They put on a good show and kept us focused to the right while they fucked us over on the left."

"They killed them, Travis," Stuart looked up at him. "Last night, in the house something went down and Jason and Quinn killed them. We lived with them for months and never saw them for what they were until they were discovered but did they have to die for it?"

"Do you really think either Jason or Quinn would have made a lethal finding if something hadn't pressed it?"

"No, but I don't get this one. Not for me. Not because she wanted to date me." He looked at Travis.

"They were trying to kill Ash, Stuart. That's why they came back. To kill her just so you wouldn't have her. Jason was with Ashley while you were gone. They told him what they were going to do. Told him he was dead, too."

Stuart only stared at him.

"Those aren't pulled muscles Jason is hiding under his shirt."

"They could have just left," Stuart said, "Why try to hurt anyone?"

"They were vampires. The bad kind."

Travis reached in his pocket and pulled out the micro cassette recorder with a set of headphones attached and handed it to Stuart

"What's this?"

"Jason had a tape-recorder on top of the remote on the TV in case it went wrong. He wanted to make sure we knew what happened and knew one of us would find it right away when we went for the remote. He recorded the whole thing."

Stuart looked at it then back up at Travis.

"It's ugly, Stuart. I mean horrifyingly ugly. And you need to listen to it. It's going to make you sick but you will know what happened last night."

"You heard it?"

"Three times. I couldn't believe it so I played it again. It's about six minutes long and Jason got them to admit everything."

Stuart reached up and took the tape recorder, picking up each ear bud and placing them in his ears. He hit play as Travis walked away.

Power Shopping

2017

A night out shopping with a girlfriend had never been high on Ashley's social calendar. In fact, anything with a girlfriend was difficult for her. When she came to the household she now called home she got a new family who took her in. She had the father to her daughter, the little girl who looked more like Ash then she should. She gave Ash twenty hugs a day minimal. Ash's life was damn near perfect.

Jason's wife, Taylor, became the little sister Ashley had craved for her whole life.

Tonight, they hit the mall after dark for a late girl's night out. They had hours to drop plastic cards down at the registers. Ash had the financial backing to buy anything she wanted, as did Taylor. They shopped and took time for lattes at a cafe in the mall and ate cinnamon rolls. They laughed, talking about their men and enjoyed the food and company.

"He doesn't think he snores," Taylor said. "Like I would make that up."

"Try putting something out of place in Stuart's room."

"That's your room, too."

Ashley looked at Taylor and smiled. "You would have to take that fact up with him after I left rings on the cabinet with my tea."

The bags they each carried had the names of Nordstrom's and Dress Me Up, the children's boutique carrying cute clothes her daughter, Charlotte, would like.

Heading out the double glass door to the parking lot, Ash carried a large pink Victoria's Secret bag. She planned on letting Ian see her purchases after they retired to their room. She planned on discussing preferences for an energetic night.

November's cool air was stronger than the sweaters, jeans and boots they each wore, sending a slow shiver up Ash's spine.

"She's going to love it," Taylor said.

Ash looked at her. "Love what?"

"The vampire costume you got in Charlotte's size."

Ash paused as they approached the car. They were driving one of Evan's rebuilds—a classic Cadillac, circa 1941. It was harder to drive than her Explorer, but hell, it was just a hoot to fire the mammoth machine up and hit the horn to hear it play the Tarzan theme.

"I wanted to get one in Jason's size," Taylor said.

Ash smiled. Getting Jason involved with anything immature wasn't so hard.

"You get him one, we'll need four more and then what will we do with the infantile side of them?"

The parking lot was an expansion of asphalt with painted lines. Theirs was the only car there. They were parked under a light. Vampire or not, girls had to be careful.

"Super soakers?" Taylor giggled.

Ash laughed, imagining and picturing it. Because it was so easy to picture them.

Taylor dropped her bags by the back of the car. Ash opened the trunk, passed off the keys to Taylor and started to pack things in. The Cadillac was a good choice. The trunk would just about hold everything.

Hearing the gasp from Taylor, Ash pulled away from the trunk to lean out to see what was up. A man, not friendly, had his ugly fingers around Taylor's upper arm.

Ash moved back behind the cover of the lifted trunk lid to think for a few seconds. A lot of days she still scrambled with a mixed up mind. Sometimes it was a challenge to know what she should be doing when.

Unless it came to her job history.

Cop and Ash, they had been meshed in a reality too strong to keep down.

Ash came out, getting few feet distance from the car in case mobility was necessary. She concentrated and stood tall and ready. Taylor stood closer to him. He whispered in her ear.

"Malls been closed for half an hour," he said to Ash. "What were you bitches still doing here?"

Ash watched him. Head shaved and skin pale. He wore the dark security shirt she had seen inside with the other mall-cop.

He wasn't a mall cop. Not with those piercings and those tats.

She gave a weak smile and let him see it. She kept her voice soft, anxious. "No," Ash whimpered. "Don't. Don't hurt her."

He tightened his hold on Taylor's arm. Taylor was still too new to her new possibilities. Her face looked a shade lighter, her eyes tearing. Ashley could see her shaking.

"Lean in," he said into Taylor's ear. "Flash the lights."

"Don't do it, Taylor," Ash said.

Taylor stopped. She pulled her hand back.

Ugly-Man snarled and shoved her out of the way. He took care of the lights while Taylor righted herself.

Almost on cue, a beat up Grand Marquis with too many miles and too many primer-painted fenders pulled up. It stopped parallel to the Cadillac.

Ugly-Man reached in his pocket and pulled out a knife to rival Quinn's. It made the same sound as Quinn's with a similar blade, but Ash wasn't worried.

"Get in the car," he said, staring straight at Taylor.

Ash might have trouble in areas of her mind that were taken out by bad guys, but she retained enough of the person she was before vampire to know step one to step two to step three.

Taylor had been raised sheltered, protected. She never had to face an all-out assault that could cripple.

Taylor moved toward the car's open back door.

"No," Ash snapped.

The second man got out of the driver's side of the Grand Marquis to lean on the top of the car. He was just as ugly, though his shirt was a red Hawaiian print. He stared at Ash. "What do you mean no? You think you decide?" He laughed and the sound was about as appealing as the rest of him.

Taylor stared at her.

Ash looked Taylor right in her eye. "Cop Law #1: Get into the car at Point A; sign up to be dead at Point B."

The driver laughed again as he moved around his car toward Ashley. "I like that. But you're no cop so get in the fucking car."

"But…we can't…" Taylor whispered. Her eyes were wide, her breath hitched.

"Gives us the upper hand in this situation, don't you think?" Ash smiled reassuringly.

Taylor dropped her gaze before looking at the men. She looked at Ash for support.

"I *suggest* you do something," Ash said.

"Did I say you could talk?" He took a step toward her in a move that was designed to look intimate. Chest out, fist clenched.

"I only practiced with Jason," Taylor told Ash. "A few times,"

"Time to put it to use."

The man in front of her reached up and grabbed Ash by the upper arm in a grip that would leave bruises. Ash didn't have the power of suggestion. It was taken from her when they came for Jason. She had other skills, though, ones she practiced in the basement with her men. If there was one thing they demanded, it was that she and Taylor were safe.

Ash kept the asshole in view. The trick here was to move toward them without looking like she had that in mind.

When Taylor turned to look straight at the man beside her, Ash moved, closing the distance between her and the driver. He was near now, close enough to matter. Ash slammed her head forward, a dead aim on positioning. She nailed him with her forehead, catching him on the bridge of his nose with a deliberate aim. Impact was hard enough to make his nose erupt in red, a yelp coming out of him. He staggered backwards, both his hands covering his face and oozing blood between the fingers.

Ash jumped back as he went to his knees.

"Oh, you bitch, I'll get you for this." His voice was garbled, sounding wet and sticky.

Ash looked at Taylor.

"Fall," Taylor said loud, with slow deliberation.

Arms flapped, his face shocked. He didn't even go to his knees as he went down flat.

"What?" he cried. "What the fuck …?"

The driver tried to stand, holding his bleeding face in both hands. Blood seeped through his fingers. Ash smelled it, as vampires do, but it didn't do anything for her. Both men were on the ground, both whining.

Ash looked at the open trunk with the packages, then back to Taylor. "Evan said you could store three bodies in it."

Taylor, still pale, almost smiled. "Are we collecting them?"

Ash laughed, soft. "I don't know what to do with them. I thought we could take them somewhere to get some advice."

"Ewe," Taylor found her giggle. "They're going to be pissed."

Ash grinned at Taylor's swearing. Getting Taylor to swear was an action they were developing at the house. It sounded real cute when she pulled it off in appropriate situations. It was probably her Southern Belle accent that made it work.

"Get them to climb in the trunk," Ash said. "Maybe our friends can teach these two manners."

Taylor stood taller. Color came back to her face. She turned to their guests.

Back at the house where the bags had to be moved to, Ash followed Taylor into the kitchen. Taylor dropped everything she was carrying on the table. The table was almost covered. Ash came up behind her, using the space left and then dropped some on the floor.

"Did you buy good, wife?" Jason smirked from the end of the dining room table not buried in bags. An almost finished piece of chocolate cake sat on his plate beside the half full glass of milk.

"I'm sure I did you proud some way," she smiled before leaning over to kiss him quick.

Ian came in the room. "You're late."

"Where's Charlotte?" Ash asked.

He pulled the baby monitor off his back pocket to show her. "Rocked her, read to her and put her to bed, all by myself." His accent still made her tingle at times.

Ash got a glass and moved to the sink for water. "We had some trouble with the car."

"What?" Evan snapped from the TV room. "You hurt the car? I'm selling that sucker."

"The car is fine," Ash said. She finished her drink and put the glass in the sink.

Ian stared at her. When she didn't answer right away, he pressed.

"What?"

She looked up at him and grinned. "We locked a couple of criminals in the trunk."

Jason's gaze came up. Ian stayed focused.

"You have criminals in our trunk?" Evan asked.

"You were right," Ash told him. "Two bodies went in fine. Three would have been easy, too."

"What?"

"Yeah," she half-smiled. "We didn't know what to do with them so we thought we'd pass them off to you."

"Pass who off to us?" Quinn asked as he came in and headed to the coffee pot.

"The criminals in her trunk."

Quinn stopped and tilted his chin. He slowly turned to face the room. "Is that as ludicrous as it sounds?"

"What else were we supposed to do with them?" Taylor asked.

"They wanted us to go for a drive with them," Ash said. "I didn't feel like it and didn't think Taylor liked the idea either. We declined and put them in the trunk."

Quinn chuckled. "You two don't look worse for wear. Where did you pick them up?"

"We didn't pick them up. They tried to pick us up. And we're fine," Ash said. "She did good, Jason. She suggested them right into the back of the car."

Jason smiled. "You did?"

Taylor nodded. "It wasn't as hard as I thought."

Ian laughed, soft. "Can we get back to the fact there are extra people in the car? We have to deal with that."

Taylor smiled. "Ash left one bloody."

"Alright," Ian said, "We can talk about that."

"Or not," Ash smiled.

He put his hands out in front of her, waiting.

"You know I don't drive," Ash said.

Ian glared at her a little before turning to Taylor. She reached into her jacket pocket and pulled out the keys, slapping them into his hand. His fingers closed over them.

He turned to the room. "I'm going to check out our newly acquired criminals. Anyone want to come?"

Quinn smiled. Evan stepped forward. Jason pushed his chair back, the chair legs grating out displeasure. Ash pulled in the satisfaction of having this home. She knew her men, knew they would make the problem go away without violence or permanent damage.

"Let's go meet them," Ian said.

Travis stepped into the room, his hair wet from his shower.

"Meet who?" he asked.

Ho Ho Ho
2017

Ian shut the fire extinguisher off while the white cloud hung thick. He leaned forward to look a little closer.

If the smell was any indication, dinner might be late.

Quinn and Jason laughed their way through the fog, waving their arms.

"Whose idea was it to deep fry the turkey?" Stuart asked.

Quinn and Jason pointed to Travis at the door. The garage reeked of a fowl gone bad.

"Good job," Stuart said, handing off the fire extinguisher with a double pat on the shoulder.

"You think this is good? Wait and see what the girls dished up," Travis said.

Ian paused, not sure if he wanted to know more about that.

The guys stood around the table, looking at the show of destroyed mess in front of them. Different colors, different textures. They only thing the dishes shared was the smell.

Travis pointed at the blackened yams and stuffing.

"The oven temp got doubled," Ash said, biting her lip.

"Hooow?" Jason whined.

"It was turned up. That's all I know," Ash said.

"The pies?" Quinn asked.

"I stored them in the mud room. There was a leak…" Taylor sighed.

"It got all the pies?"

"It was a big leak," Taylor said. "Quinn got it under control."

"Jason and Quinn set fire to the turkey. And we lost part of the house," Ian said.

"It's fixable." Quinn said, trying to hide his smirk.

"Christmas dinner is looking less likely."

Ash pointed. "We have the vegetables. And the bread."

Jason started laughing first. Quinn next. Then Evan, covering his mouth as he chuckled.

Jason pulled out his phone and played with the buttons.

"How does Chinese sound?"

"For Christmas," Taylor gasped. "But I made Cranberry Corned Bread."

"We can put it on the side." He leaned over, kissing his wife.

Half an hour later, he helped take all the bags to the kitchen. He put them on the still set table.

Traditions were fluid, Ian thought. Even ones as important as this. Watching his wife lean over the high chair to help his daughter eat noodles, he smiled. Wife and daughter, two things he had not thought he would ever achieve. Not after his life in Scotland. He hadn't thought he would get this lucky.

Travis leaned over to kiss Charlotte on her brown hair. He brought his gaze up to Ian's.

"She's a lot cuter than you."

The voices mixing in conversation and laughter made isolation difficult. Ian kept up.

"But your wife is still hot."

"Stop staring at my wife."

She smiled as she looked at Ian. "I don't mind," she grinned.

Ian laughed at her. "Stop staring at Travis."

"I'll stare at her," Jason said.

"Excuse me?" Taylor asked him.

Ian enjoyed watching Jason try to cover his lack of judgment in speaking up.

He toasted with his sake, complements of a full cellar, and thought for only a second about the meals they had back home with the Scottish family. He had left behind the idea of celebrating in Scotland ever again for the Christmas they had found here.

Chinese food was unusual.

Ian smiled, shooting the sake. Ash came closer. His hand snaked around her waist, pulling her close enough for her hands to rest on his chest.

"Christmas was ruined," she said.

He reached to the table and picked up an egg roll, dipping its end into sweet and sour. He held it up for her to bite.

"Food was ruined. Not the holiday. Open."

She did and he put the egg roll between her teeth.

"Travis," Stuart snapped. "Name the one thing that makes it Christmas?"

"Beside the tree?" Evan interjected.

"Besides that," Stuart smiled.

"Wreath?"

"Reindeers?"

"Presents."

"Whole house smells like pumpkin shit," Evan said.

Ash sniffed while Charlotte smeared her food on the white plastic tray. More of them covered her hair and the floor.

"I smell ginger and onions." Ash said.

Travis smiled. "And that would be Christmas," he said.

Ash unbuckled Charlotte and let the mess smear on her front. "Come on, Baby Girl. I'll clean you up."

She walked to the hall and upstairs for baby-duty.

Stuart watched her until she disappeared.

"Presents tomorrow," Travis said, next to him.

"After the ones tonight," Stuart said.

"Is it worth the wait?"

Stuart leaned back in his chair and looked up at Travis.

Travis stared back. "You waited long enough."

"I think I waited the exact right amount of time."

"We were wired different from the moment we were turned. Even in our shittiest times, we searched for a way to do it different, to do it right. We found us..."

~Jason Sullivan

ABOUT THE AUTHOR

Award-winning author, Jacqui Jacoby lives and writes in the beauty of Northern Arizona. Currently adjusting to being an empty nester with her first grandchild to draw her pictures, Jacqui is a self-defense hobbyist. Having studied martial arts for numerous years she retired in 2006 from the sport, yet still brings strength she learned from the discipline to her characters. She is a working writer, whose career includes writing books, novellas & short stories, teaching online & live workshops and penning short nonfiction. Hobbies include forensics, aromatherapy and remembering the people who passed before.

Follow her at www. jacquijaxjacoby.com

http://jaxsmovielist.blogspot.com/

Twitter: JaxJacoby

Facebook: Jacqui Jax Jacoby

Google + Jacqui Jacoby

THE DEAD MEN

ALSO BY JACQUI JACOBY

NOW AVAILABLE

Dead Men Play the Game

Magic Man

Bystander

Dead Men Seal the Deal

Illegal Exit: a novella

Aaden's Hope

COMING OUT IN 2018

Dead Men Feel the Heat

Silent Echos

Retribution

Silent Echos

Available 2018

PROLOGUE

Laying back on the stacked pillows, Davis James pulled a smoke out of the stale pack that had been dislodged in today reorganizational. With the lighter he had in his wooden junk box on the shelf in his side of the closet—they were both his sides now. He thought as his flipped the Zippo to life.

It had been ten years since his last smoke.

Inhaling now, he coughed some and then really got the full impact of the cigarette.

And it sucked.

He coughed some more as he smoked it down another half inch not ready to admit how much he hated the stench and taste.

The clock neared three a.m.

In the dark, as he sipped at the Jacks in his juice glass, he could see her empty drawers still pulled open.

Hence the forgotten pack found.

The closet door ajar, he could make out the shape of three left coat hangers in a void of empty space.

The two guns he cleaned tonight—the ones that hadn't need cleaning—they sat on the night stand beside his wallet and keychain. The key chain was made out of black tourmaline stone, almost two inches in length. It was carefully wrapped in decorated copper wire to keep it safe. He stared at it. It was something he always had but rarely thought about.

It must work, though. He had been carrying it since college and hadn't died on the job yet. He didn't buy into the 'protection' angle of the crystal.

The person who made it for him believed in its powers and that alone had kept it in his pocket even when he was with Angela.

"Where did you get it?" Angela had asked once.

"My God-daughter made it."

Which was a lie.

It was the God daughter's mother, before the God daughter had even been born, who did this kind act for the simple reason she had cared about him.

Meghan. On a night he should pick up the phone and call to see if Angela wanted to meet and talk, Meghan was on his mind.

It wasn't a shock she had moved out at all after eleven months of living-in-sin.

He hadn't loved her. She knew that.

She hadn't loved him.

He knew that, too.

It just felt weird tonight to be in the house alone after all those months together with the stone on the keychain drawing his attention. Looking down, he found the cigarette replaced in his fingers with the keychain when he hadn't even realized he made the move.

Angela had been gone fourteen hours. Her text said she was moving back east to take a job in Georgetown.

And he should be thinking about that and not the conversation that led him rubbing the crystal he held in his hand.

"You pick the stone," Meg had said when she was twenty. The stone had been in her growing collection of crystals and rocks. And this in his hand had been the one he picked when she had been blindfolded.

Sex and Angela, they did that well, even as the relationship was failing. Favorite TV show to share? They never agreed. Movies? Nope. Meals were good as they both cooked. Conversations, though?

He took a long drink trying to remember her sister's boyfriend's name. He should know. They had met enough times. And he worked for the damn FBI. Shouldn't Davis remember something like that?

Greg?

Craig?

Michael?

The bottle of Jacks was a lot lower than tomorrow's desk time allowed. The smoke smoldered on a small dish.

Angela and he, they had barely said a word to each other in three months. They hadn't even taken time to fight about that.

But the sex, he thought again, had still been good. Making him feel tonight as if maybe he should have questioned how they had gone at it mindlessly.

Wearing only his grey pajama bottoms, his chest bare except for the tattoo starting on his shoulder and moving down his bicep, he didn't feel the chill in the October air, not even when Angela had tuned the heat down when she left.

The TV on the wall across from him blinked on, setting to Pandora. The blue screen cast shadows on the walls around him. It wasn't so much the spookiness of the fact the remote was beside the TV and not him as it was downright eerie when the music started to play.

Tom Petty's *Listen to Her Heart*. Not the station he usually set. As for the words, they clicked off in his head, shifting his thoughts from Angela to Meg.

Closing his eyes, he took a deep breath through his nose, letting it out, the stale smoke still in his head.

"Davis…"

He heard it but not with his ears. A feeling he hadn't felt in a long time traveled over his skin, feather soft. He shivered at the sudden cold, opening his eyes. When the TV screen across from the bed fogged, he sat up, wrists on his knees.

The word *contúirt* drew itself into the mist, staying long enough to be memorized before it slipped away from the glass.

Davis swung his legs over the side, his feet on the ground. He grabbed a gun, wrapped his hands around the butt and moved to the doorway.

The wood floors cooled his soles. From the door he could see down the hall. At the turn to the living room, the light leaned toward serious while still hitting melodramatic.

He swung into the room, his arms raised, obstructed by the superimposed image of a blue tone bedroom.

"Shit," he whispered, taking in the whole picture across from him, from the night stands to closet door to a figure lying on the bed.

She was sound asleep on her side, totally unaware of what her mind conjured.

He wasn't psychic.

She was. Times ten at least.

This was her dream coming to him.

"Davis…"

He heard it again. She hadn't moved. The voice hadn't come from her.

Her hair was still red but even without that he would have known it was her. His body and mind had craved her presence since the day he walked away.

No offense, Angela.

Breathing heavy, he lowered the gun, still held in both hands. He was afraid to move and shatter the image that seemed as solid as the house.

"Meg," he said.

She stirred a little but didn't wake.

"Meghan," he snapped louder.

Before she could answer, his gaze shot up to the two shadows on the wall, sliding down. Black in color, the texture unsure. They moved toward her.

"Meghan," he shouted. "Wake up Now!"

www.ingramcontent.com/pod-product-compliance
Lightning Source LLC
Chambersburg PA
CBHW060212180626
46813CB00007B/2801